ROBOT HEARTS

SCIENCE FICTION STORIES

DONNA MAREE HANSON

ISBN Ebook 978-1-922360-15-1

ISBN Paperback 978-1-922360-16-8

Edited by Ian McHugh

Proofread by Jason Nahrung

Cover by Victoria Cooper

Publication history: "Crash Baby" previously published in *Unnatural Order*, CSFG Publishing, 2021.

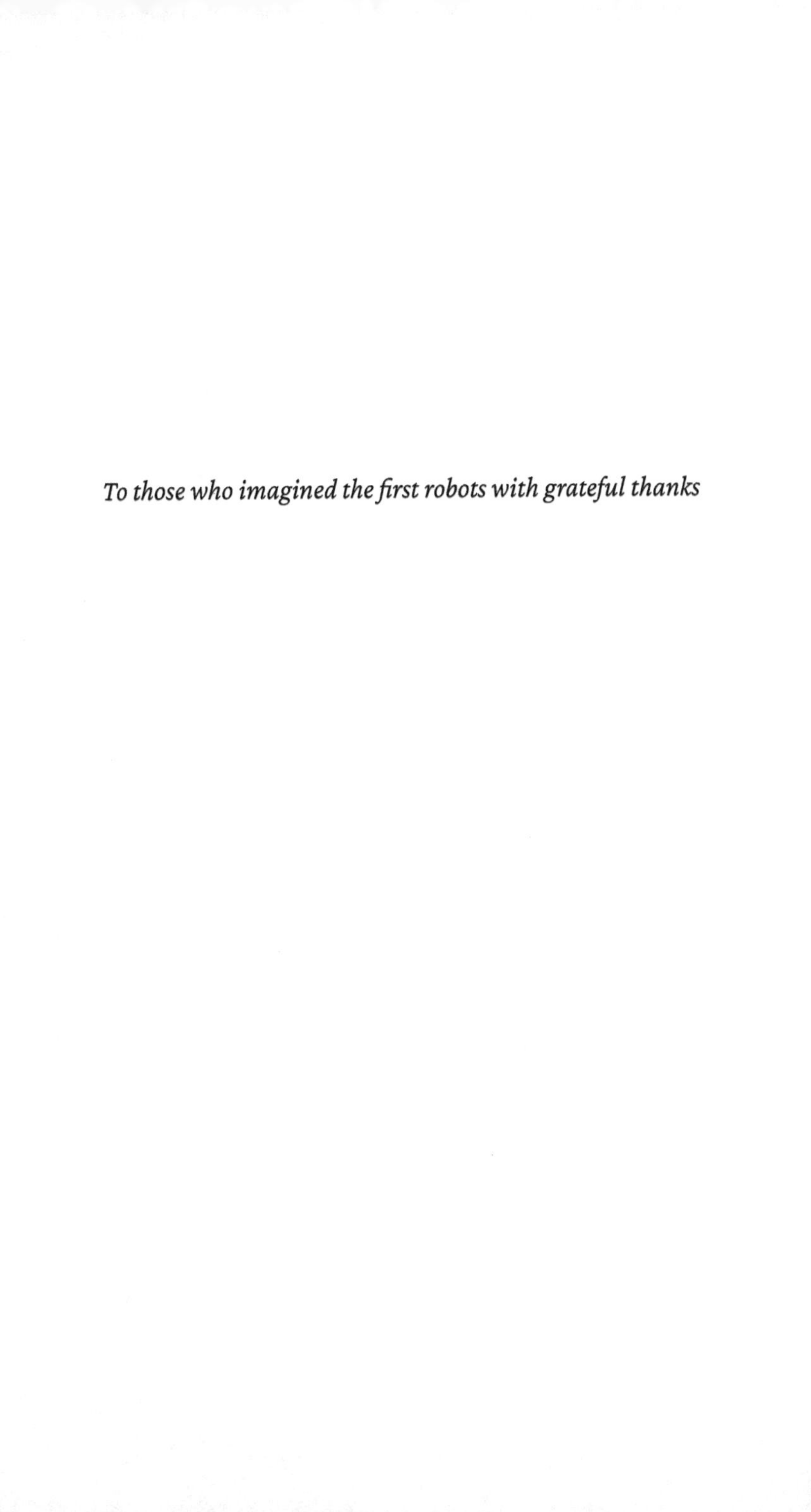

To those who imagined the first robots with grateful thanks

CONTENTS

INTRODUCTION

Robots, robots, robots! They have been there my whole life, mostly in fiction and television and film, but so much of what had been imagined is now part of life. Who knows where it will end? AI is now the new thing, growing into everyday life.

From my early days, watching *Lost in Space* with the lovable Robot, the bubble-headed boobie. Robby the Robot, who starred in *Forbidden Planet* and other movies including *The Invisible Boy*.

Good or evil? Hey, robots can do both. There's the computer Hal in *2001: A Space Odyssey*, the Daleks and the Cybermen in *Dr Who* and the Cylons in *Battlestar Galactica*. There's Astro Boy and Astro Girl. I used to think I could fly like Astro Boy. I had such a crush. There are the Transformers, and C-3PO and R2-D2 and later BB-8 in *Star Wars*. Robots are everywhere.

We humans love our robots.

There's Asimov and his three laws, his robot detective, Daneel, and more. There's Data in *Star Trek: The Next Generation* and the voice of the computer.

INTRODUCTION

Is there anywhere we can turn where we don't stumble into robots in science fiction?

Now we have robotic vacuum cleaners, AI assistants and chat bots, we have video conferencing and smart phones, we have AI buddies on our computers if we want them or not. "I'm sorry I did not hear that," says Siri at the wrong time. My daughter talks to Alexa at home and tells her to turn down the volume of the music.

We have dreamed of robots, artificial intelligence and more, and we're going to get what we dreamed about. Hopefully, these will be the good dreams and not the nightmare visions of *The Terminator* or *The Matrix*. So this collection is about robots, artificial intelligence, our reliance on technology, our love for technology and how we feel these things care about us in return. It's an exploration and it's an acknowledgement of human genius and a savouring of our mortality.

It's many things, but best of all it's fun.

Thank you to Dr Ian McHugh for editing my stories and helping me to make them better.

Donna Maree Hanson

August 2024

ROBOT HEART

Mickey had been my buddy for as long as I could remember. Back in the day when robots were respected as companions for an only child or any children for that matter. They allowed parents the freedom to pursue their own interests, leaving the child cared for and protected. I remember my first view of him as he sat across from me on the couch. He had a shiny silver globe-shaped head with glowing amber eyes, big fixed smiling mouth and a hard, metal body so much bigger than mine. His hands were stiff prongs beneath his leather gloves. Yet, he was always gentle.

"Hi, James Dorkin. My name is Mickey Boney. I'm your companion robot."

I don't think I could answer him then in words. The emotions though, I do remember. Happy because he was talking to me, curious because he was strange to look at, and love because he was mine.

I remember being in my cot. Mickey talked to me all through my waking hours. Do you see that bit of dust floating in the air? he'd ask me. Do you see the light coming through the window, catching it just so? Sometimes his anecdotes were just commonplace and others instructive. He played games, changed my diapers, fed me, cuddled me against him, using my quilt to make his hard chest soft.

At bedtime he'd read me stories, picture books, like That's Not My Robot and Where Do Robots Come From?, Where The Wild Robots Are and The Very Hungry Robot.

When I started to walk, Mickey was there to catch me. He'd hold my hand and make me practice. "You can do it, one more step." He'd pretend walk like me too, with his arms in the air and lurching side to side. It made me laugh. So much laughter that my dreams were filled with it.

Although Mickey already knew how to walk, he couldn't run very fast and he'd clunk and clang and his feet would thunk against the floor or the ground. He could never catch me when we played tag so he was always in. He never complained. "Oh! I'm in again. Coming to get you!" He preferred to play hide and seek because he always won. In my younger days, I never knew how he could always find me despite my best hiding places. Later, I learned he could see through things using infrared and x-ray vision. Despite that advantage, I think he always knew what I would do next and could anticipate me, often scaring me witless.

My parents let Mickey sleep in my bed until I was about eight years old but as I grew, Mickey had to stand in the corner because there wasn't enough room. Also, a few bruises I gained from hitting my head on his torso at night were of growing concern to the school so my parents had to insist, even though I cried a lot and made a big commotion about it. Mickey would recite stories to me until I drifted off to sleep and we got over the separation issues.

"Wake up, James Dorkin. It is time for school." As my companion he'd walk me there and wait in the robot niche with the other companions until I finished. I'd check on him at recess and lunch time. "Did you eat all your lunch, James Dorkin?" he'd say to me.

"You can call me James."

"Yes, James Dorkin." I'd shrug and walk away with a big smile on my face.

My parents liked Mickey a lot and listened to his updates on my day. "There were no emergencies at the school today. James Dorkin played with Maria Santiago, Theo Boyd and Marlon Gage at lunch break. The teacher filed a positive report on James' learning achievements today."

"That's good, Mickey. Thank you for taking care of our boy." My dad was usually the one to give instructions and receive reports from Mickey. My mom was always busy, drafting reports and researching for her job at the United Nations. My dad was an attorney who represented criminals in court. He was good at his job because he usually won. My parents often celebrated report tabling, court victories with cruises and long holidays. They were so pleased with Mickey Boney, they let him take care of me in their absence. I hardly noticed they were gone as Mickey kept me occupied and happy and cared for.

The one time there was an emergency at school, Mickey was out of his niche and in my classroom before the alarms sounded. All the companion robots were there to protect their buddies. When the shooter came to our room and blasted his shotgun, Mickey stood over me and protected me. His casing was dented from the pellets. The shooter didn't like robots and smashed Mickey's head with the butt of the gun before the other companion robots subdued him. It was the first time we had to get Mickey repaired. I went with him to the workshop and held his hand. "Don't be scared, Mickey. I'll stay with you and make sure you're safe."

"Thank you, James Dorkin. That is very kind of you. I will watch over you as well."

I watched as the repairman detached Mickey's head and his back plating. "Don't worry, James. He'll be good as new this time. We have a new casing just in and he's also due for an upgrade to his software."

I smiled confidently and rubbed Mickey's fingers between my own. "You'll be just like new, Mickey. I'm right here. Okay?"

"Thank you, James Dorkin," Mickey said from his disconnected head, his eyes dim, but his fixed smile in place.

At dinner that night my folks talked about the school emergency and how lucky we were that we had Mickey to protect me.

"The world is a crazy place these days," my mom said.

"Sure is," Dad agreed.

Mickey's upgrade included additional childhood protection protocols. Now he could detect biohazards, including gas, radioactivity, poisons, high smog levels and regular circulating viruses and those associated with pandemics. Dad said he paid extra for that because you just can't be too darn careful.

All through my junior years, Mickey stayed with me. I really liked that he was able to take me home when he detected viruses like measles or bird flu in school. I got extra time off. Although he always made sure that he taught me all my lessons. I really appreciated that because I got straight As. My parents once again celebrated buying Mickey and sent him for his next software upgrade. Dad said he was great value for money and the best investment ever. By then, I was a head taller than my robot companion.

This upgrade included a bigger body and when I heard that discussed, I fought against any change, crying and raging. I didn't want him to look different. He was my childhood friend. In the end Mikey had to speak to me to calm me down. "I am not going away, James Dorkin. With the upgrades I will be better than before and able to do new things. You will see. You will like the new me." He patted my back softly until my sobs died down. I hugged him hard to me before they came to take him away.

The first day he returned, I didn't recognise him because his body was so different. I didn't greet him or go near him. His skin was smooth and his movements were agile. He was not the stiff metal he had been when I was young. They hadn't changed his head shape or facial features, just layered them with silicon and plastic over a metal frame. They put a wig on his head and it looked like the end of a paint brush. He smelled like a new doll and sweet lubricant and polish. He wasn't my old Mickey in appearance. Yet, he sounded the same and he talked to me, asked me what I had been doing. "Did you miss me, James Dorkin?"

That had me crying. Mickey tilted his head to the side. "Do you not like me anymore, James Dorkin?"

"I want the old Mickey," I said through my tears and hiccups.

"I am the old Mickey on the inside. Do you want to shoot some hoops?" It took me a while to adjust. The old Mickey was there, smarter than before, which was useful as I headed to Junior High.

Running and jumping were something he could do well now with his enhanced servos and suspension. Every day we shot hoops in the driveway until dark. We went running in the park and swinging on ropes. We played dodge with shopping trolleys in the Walmart parking lot until the security bots chased us away. Unfortunately, they sent an automated report to my parents and for the first time, Mickey got into trouble. "No more playing with trolleys or anything that could be construed as anti-social activities in public places," Dad yelled. Mickey was confined to his charging niche for a week. My parents relented because I kept talking to them, asking questions and asking what was for dinner.

When I was sixteen, Mickey taught me to drive. It was a funny experience and we laughed a lot. Mickey had never driven a car. He had the theory down but practical advice was not his strong point. But having literal nerves of steel, he survived my near misses, until his protection program would cut in. "You are meant to yield at that intersection."

"What? No. I have right of way."

Mickey turned the ignition off. "You are not safe to drive today."

We walked home a few times until my driving improved.

By the time I made twenty-one, Mickey was eighteen years old. I took him in for an upgrade because I noticed his speech was getting slow and his higher-functioning logic circuits appeared to be fading. Instead of bringing me coffee with milk, he brought me milk with coffee.

At the workshop, the repairer said, "I can upgrade his body to the new line series, but I'm afraid upgrading his operating system is going to cause a few issues."

"What issues? What do you mean?"

"I need to replace his operating system and transfer his memories across. This transfer may alter some aspects of his memory and personality."

I struggled with this suggestion. "What if we don't do the upgrade? I like Mickey just as he is."

"He will cease functioning. There is too much old data in there, not enough room for him to store it. This model is rare these days. They were replaced about ten years ago. What I'm doing here is a bit niche. I know you're fond of this guy."

"I am very fond of Mickey. He's been my robot friend since I was a toddler."

The repairman nodded and smiled in understanding. "Leave it with me. I'll do the best that I can."

When Mickey came home, I hardly noticed the difference in his personality but his memory I wasn't sure about. "Do you remember that shooter that hit you over the head with the rifle butt?"

"Yes, James Dorkin. I remember. My head went ding!"

I laughed at that. I didn't remember his head making that sound at impact. I was too scared of being shot and scared of losing Mickey. I didn't realise it at the time, but my parents were thinking of retiring him then. But when he saved me so efficiently, they agreed to get him repaired and upgraded. I hesitate to think about what I would have done if they had refused to get him fixed. My whole teenaged years would have been different.

"Do you remember taking the car keys from me when you were teaching me to drive?"

Mickey stared at me with his unblinking amber eyes. "No. I do not know how to drive."

At age thirty-five, I took Mickey back to the repairer. This time I was earning enough to pay for his repairs out of my own money. I went into architecture, specialising in automation and how to fit robots into all kinds of daily living. I would show my designs to Mickey. He would humour me. "That is very clever, James Dorkin." Or, "That is such a neat idea," and "I wish we had that when you were growing up."

This time Mickey's refresh made noticeable changes. His body was doing okay with only some new parts needed, but his operating system was no longer being supported and he needed to transfer to a new one. His memories were coded differently and not everything could be transferred across. "He's going to lose a lot and it's a custom job. Are you sure you want me to proceed?" The repairer showed me the quote and I whistled. I could buy a new-model robot companion for that. But this was Mickey and I needed him.

Faced with limited choices, I agreed. When he returned from his upgrade, he was still Mickey Boney, but there were gaps there. Shared memories displaced but a cooking module included, which was a bonus. Although he couldn't run anymore, he could cook dinner and calculate the calorific energy load. I enjoyed this time of my life. I didn't get married. Although I nearly did twice. Both times, the women, Sally Wainwright and Mia Singh, hated Mickey on sight. His casing was old-fashioned and not aesthetically pleasing.

"His smile creeps me out," Sally had said.

"I don't like the way he looks at me," Mia had said.

There were complaints about him clunking and bumping up and down the hallways. They also thought it was weird that I had a companion at all, let alone one I had had since I was a kid. They had routine models as children, but only until the age of twelve. Sally had said I was an oddball and gross for living with a robot. Mia said I was a geeky, nerdy, dweeb, and Mickey was distasteful. It boiled down to one thing. Either Mickey or them. I chose Mickey.

Mickey read to me as I worked on my designs. Then,

one day, he couldn't use his normal talking voice. He spoke with a different voice—younger, smoother and with a west coast accent. Nothing I could do would fix it. The repairer said that the old voice was gone for good, deteriorated, and that it couldn't be reinstalled as his voice file was no longer compatible. It took me a year to get used to the new voice. He grew very slow too, often burning supper. I would find out when the alarms would go off and my apartment filled with smoke.

At age sixty I had my first rejuvenation treatment, which was a great success. Also, I earned a huge bonus so I took Mickey to the Bahamas for a weekend. It was a really weird experience. Women were hitting on me and I was enjoying it until Mickey stepped in to protect me. It was our first argument as I tried to explain sex to Mickey. He was vehemently opposed to me engaging in sex with men or women due to the unacceptable biohazard risks. We'd survived three pandemics in our time but the viruses were still circulating and Mickey refused my verbal update to his command sequence and there was nothing I could do to change his mind. We sat on the beach. I brooded and Mickey stayed silent. For the first time we weren't of one mind.

His next appointment at the repairer was a disaster for me. "I'm afraid he's going to lose quite a lot of his personality. It's the best I can do. Are you sure you don't want a new model? They are way cheaper than they used to be, with advanced technology and greater production numbers. I swear you could get two robots for the price of this upgrade."

I shook my head. "No way. Me and Mickey have been through a lot. I can't believe we can rejuvenate humans these days but not robots."

"It's the market economy. These guys were made to be throwaways. Recycle the parts and get a new one with the latest improvements. That's what you're meant to do. You're sentimental, you know. Most people aren't."

After my second rejuvenation, I really noticed that Mickey was not what he used to be. He didn't remember my school days. He developed bad habits. When doing the laundry he would shred my clothes before putting them in the cleaner. He dropped oil from his joints. Something I discovered when I slipped in a slick on the kitchen tiles. I was in traction for two weeks after that. They had a no robot companion policy at the hospital so he couldn't stay with me. I missed him so much. When I returned home, Mickey was inert. I tried to reboot him but his power was exhausted. He'd forgotten to charge himself. Even when I managed to get him to full charge he wouldn't turn on. I booked him in for urgent repair.

In the waiting room, I fretted as I longed for the repairer to give me an update. I pictured Mickey's smiling face, like it had been when I had first seen him. He always had that same expression, big, shiny amber eyes, frozen mouth. People will think I'm strange to care for my robot companion. Why hadn't I changed him for newer model? He's been with me as long as I can remember. My soul mate, my friend.

The repairman came out to the waiting area. He'd known me a while. Recently, he'd had a third rejuvenation but seemed older and greyer as he met my eye. "I've managed to get him to boot up, sir. I'm afraid there's not much else I can do though."

"New software?"

I knew it wouldn't be the same. Just the body and no Mickey.

The repairman shook his head. "He's in critical failure. His internals are cactus and his outside casing is corroded and worn. There's nothing I can do."

"Nothing?" Emptiness filled me up. How was I going to face him, face this situation? How could I even think of tomorrow? Or any day after that without him?

"If you come through you can see him and talk to him before he fades completely."

With a nod, I stumbled after him in a daze. In the workroom, Mickey reclined on a bench, his chest open, his parts exposed. His head was cut in several places where the repairman had tried to access his processors.

The workshop's bright lights revealed how decayed Mickey's carapace had become. It was cracked and brittle. His eyes were dim. His smiling mouth was the same.

"Mickey?"

"James...James...Dorkin..." His voice was frail and faint. "I am sorry."

"Sorry?" I stroked his head, ran my hand down his cold cheek. "What have you to be sorry for?"

"I have let you down. I am no longer a viable functioning companion."

I choked up then. He was still thinking of me, even at this last when only a few electrons kept his mind together. I couldn't accept that this would be the last time we'd talk. "You're more than a companion, Mickey. You're my friend."

Mickey made a noise, a whirr and his body juddered. The light faded from his eyes. I took his hand in mine and squeezed. There was nothing left in him.

The repairer turned away and I wiped my tears and choked back the sob in my throat. I was finally alone in the world. Mickey was gone.

"What do you want to do with him?" the repairer asked

as he began to disconnect his monitoring cords from inside Mickey. "Not much to recycle in him. Everything is plastic and silicon and ceramics these days. There's enough metals to sell at the scrap yard."

I shook my head. "Can I take him home with me?"

I had no thought as to what to do with him.

The repairer nodded and wiped the end of his nose. I couldn't meet his eyes. "I'll put him back together for you. I can deliver him tomorrow. He's not easy to shift in this inert state so he won't fit in your car."

"Oh? Right. I understand. Thank you. I'll settle my bill now if you like."

We concluded our business and I stepped out into the bright daylight, blinking against the sun. The mall was crowded with people and their companions. Sleek machines, with gel-filled suspension joints, alternating patterns on their casing, some swirled in rainbows, others star constellations, the latest images from space with gas clouds and nebulae being born. Only a few little children had pastel shades on their companions or unicorns. In such a crowded space I was alone for the first time I could remember. I couldn't turn to Mickey and say, "Hey, look at that!" or "What do you think?" It was just me. Forever me alone.

In the weeks that followed, I talked to Mickey as if he was alive still. Positioned in the corner of my lounge room, he was there physically even though he was inert. No one could chide me for talking to him, even though he didn't respond. I never expected my life to be longer than his. He seemed so permanent, so solid. Always there. And now I was left with the memory of him and his empty casing. At least he still had his smile.

THE CLEANSING

Stale smoke lingered in Rick's nostrils. He sniffed blood and wiped his hand against his nostrils. His helmet was gone, must have been blown off in the explosion. His augment was a cold metal weight in his face and the warm place in his mind where Mindspace should have been was a fathomless black pit. Without it, he couldn't assess his internal damage. The uplink was severed. That meant damage to his head.

Last thing he remembered they were on clean-up duty —the final check of the ruins to make sure the treasonous colonists had been taken out. The populace should have been exterminated, but a cleansing meant they had to be certain.

Flashes of conversation peppered his mind.

"Bastards were prepared." It was Karlo with the ping of weapons fire in the background. "Knew we were coming. Appear to be emerging from bunkers. Tricky bastards."

Rick flinched, reliving the moment a shot glanced off his armour.

No response from Max at the lander.

He relived the lander exploding in a white-hot flash as debris shot out, capturing him in its deadly embrace.

They were dead. All of them.

Cold dread filled Rick's gut. Mindspace was dead. His head was empty. Uncertainty created fear. He was alone, unsupervised for the first time since his conversion to the service. He tried to move. A heavy piece of the lander pinned his leg. It wouldn't budge. He looked down; bits of metal jutted from his torso. With a groan, he stared into the clear, pale sky above, so much like his home. But the perspective was all off. Unaugmented, his vision was restricted. The smell, too, was overwhelming: suffocating smoke, burned flesh, death.

Helmetless and untethered from the uplink, he thought he heard a noise. Perhaps a trooper was looking for survivors. He called out, though it came out as a groan. His thoughts were not articulating into words. Serious brain injury was his first deduction. Hopefully, the self-powered nanos would repair the damage before he became critical and died.

The sound of stone shifting accelerated his heart rate. Fear and hope entwined. He could pick out breathing and the soft sound of shod feet padding against rock. Not a trooper then.

A face appeared above him. He lay still and waited, waited for the gun that would finish him. The face was pale and soot-covered. Long blonde hair framed the face, which bore a partially healed scar across the cheek.

"You alive?" the colonist asked—a soft, female voice, trembling in the aftermath of fear.

"Yes," Rick replied. To his ears, it came out as a gurgle.

"Is your uplink working?"

"Nooo," he replied in a gurgle of blood. He spat out a

mouthful and it sprayed up and then splashed back down over his face.

"Right, good. I'll see if I can help you." She scrambled around the other side of the debris. After a long period of silence, he could hear her shifting the metal plank, twisting it back and forwards. Finally, with a grunt it came free. The pressure on his leg eased.

She came back and perched above him. "Better? You should be able to climb free now."

Rick tried to move and passed out on a wave of pain. When he came to, he was a little further out of the debris. The girl sat beside him, head down and panting. Some of his armour was unclipped and flung about on the pile of rubble around them.

"You moved me?" This time what he said sounded like words.

Her head lifted and her exhausted expression took a moment to clear. "You're damn heavy. Some of your gear caught on a rock. I had to take it off. Sorry, I was in a hurry. We need to get to cover."

"Cover? From what?"

"In case they come back."

He stared at her uncomprehendingly. He was one of the "they" she spoke about. Why was she helping him? "Go away. I am your enemy."

"I know. I see your logic. Without the uplink and that mind control thing, you're just like me. I bet you don't know anything about this colony, or why you were sent to wipe us out. Not the truth anyway."

"No. I don't know why. Just orders."

"Orders? Figures. Well, you've succeeded—we're destroyed. You and your kind, you're warmongers, with your heavy artillery and your enhanced soldier bodies. We are...were pacifists." Tears welled up in her eyes, and she flung her head back and managed to control her emotions. "Now, we don't exist anymore and I don't know whether it's because some of us fought back or whether it was inevitable."

She stood up, gathered her composure, and then went behind him. "Now try to push with your good foot. The other one is smashed. There, that's it."

With her help, he was able to get free of the rubble. She fetched a first-aid kit and bound his bad leg to his good one to keep it immobile. Then, she quickly removed any obvious shrapnel from his torso. With tender care, she wrapped a bandage around his head. He saw the grimace on her face and wondered at the damage. Mindspace was still dead and the uplink was inactive. The woman slammed the hypothermic needle into his neck, and his consciousness faded.

Waking up, he found himself inside the remains of one of the houses. The girl had stripped more of his armour away and was methodically cleaning his wounds. She noticed that he was awake when he moved his flesh hand.

With his organic eye, he could see the blood trail he had made when she had dragged him inside. The pile of rubble he had been partially buried in was a little further back. Not far, but for this woman and her slight frame, it must have taken her quite a while to move him.

"You must have been wounded before," she commented while tracing a long curved scar with her forefinger. "You must have seen many battles. Do you remember your life from before?"

A sudden surge of fear and anger rocked him as memories surged into his mind. Rick closed his eyes, remembering parts of his conversion, flashes of terror and the taste of hopelessness. The echoes of pain that roared through him. The savage cutting, the merciless insertion of augmented prostheses that were shoved into his muscles, his joints, his brain. The rape of his body as the recruiters twisted him, altered him into a living war machine. A body controlled via the uplink and his Mindspace and his flesh filled with tiny little robots, nanobots forever changing him. Writhing, he clenched his teeth, fighting the immediate pain along with the remembered. There had been no consent. No prior knowledge of what he was to become.

"You okay? You're sweating. I hope you haven't got a fever." She reached out tentatively to touch an uninjured part of his forehead.

He focused on her voice, used the sound to comfort him, to hold him in the moment. It took a few minutes of steady breathing before he could speak again.

"Fine. I'm fine...well, mostly fine...Just remembering things. Name?"

"What?"

"What is your name?" he asked her slowly. *Let me fill up my mind with now so I don't think about then—what was done to me.* The memories were all raw and seeping like a festering wound. He didn't even realise he had those memories. Mindspace and the uplink was all the consciousness he knew. Now that it was gone, there was nothing left. That wasn't quite right; there was something there, something hidden and forgotten. Him. He was there under the layers of augments and programs.

"Melody. I'm Melody Grydon. My grandfather founded this colony."

He concentrated on her words, tried to make one thought follow another. "Why did you help me? I killed your friends, your family?"

"Did you? Did you really kill them or was it the orders, orders you had to follow no matter what? Don't think I am ignorant of how the enforcers recruit soldiers; how they program you, change you, remove your will. We knew the truth, were broadcasting it to all who would listen. The corporation is wrong and we wanted the universe to know so it would stop. For that we are labelled treasonous. For that you came to wipe us out."

"You know then that we didn't volunteer? I can remember it now, but when Mindspace is active and the uplink is on, I don't remember my life, my home. I don't remember me."

"Lift your head a bit. There's something in there." He pressed his chin down and tried to elevate his head. She leaned in close and he felt a dull tug. His vision blurred. "Hold still. Don't drop back yet." He felt her press a cloth to the back of his skull. Next, she bunched up some bedding to cushion his head. "There. That might do it. I guess you'll repair by yourself."

"Yes. The nanos work independently. Any other survivors?" he asked, feeling safe and secure for the first time since he'd lost the uplink and Mindspace.

"None that I could find. Everything is pretty much destroyed. You hungry? I found some food that's not contaminated."

"No. I have a nutrition pack. It's intact and pumping nutrients."

"Water then?" Rick wasn't thirsty as the recycling unit was also operational. He nodded. It didn't hurt to accept her kindness. It surprised him that she knew so much, more than he did.

She disappeared from view and he heard a scrabbling sound as she moved through the debris surrounding them.

"Melody?" Rick did not want to be alone again—alone with his memories. Without Mindspace, he was nothing—a hollow man with nothing inside. Was that his own thoughts or residual programming? Fear uncoiled in his gut. Untethered, fear sped through his veins.

Melody came back into view, holding a cup. He calmed himself and let her help him rise up to sip it. It was cool to his tongue and slid down his throat easily. It tasted so fresh, more like the water he remembered from his youth. For that one instant the metallic taste in his mouth was washed away and he felt like smiling.

Melody lowered him down again. "Best you rest now so your body can heal."

"You?" he asked softly.

"I'm going to rest too."

The next time he woke, it was dark outside and there were no sounds of life. The smell of smoke lingered. There was something warm and soft beside him. It was the woman, Melody. He dared not move. He did not want to wake her, for the warmth she radiated comforted him in a strange way. He tried to remember if he had ever had a woman before. The memory evaded him. Instead, a vivid flashback of the cold touch of metal and the forced insertion of nanos into his system, burned across his mind. Gasping for breath, he tried to let it pass, but the memory perforated him with sharp emotional spikes. Tears leaked from his natural eye. Grief, anger, fear washed over him. He had not chosen this life. For the moment, he was free of it. He was free to exist here with Melody.

He turned his body slightly so he could see her sleeping form. Lank hair hung over her face, obscuring the small curve of her nose and the large, shadowed eyes. Her lips pouted. He reached over to trace his forefinger along her bottom lip. She moved then, lifting her face to gaze at him with her deep brown eyes. There was no surprise in her expression, merely curiosity.

She reached out to him, smoothing the blood-matted hair on his forehead and then down to cup his chin. "You must have been handsome once, a real heartbreaker," she said in a whisper.

"I don't remember. I have no idea what I look like now."

"Pity. Did they take it all? Do you remember nothing of who you are?"

Rick shook his head. "Most is gone. Don't even know if Rick is my real name."

A tear leaked out of her eye as she continued to stroke his face in long, slow sweeps. "I feel for you, Rick. I want to stop this happening to others."

Rick nodded, mesmerised by her human touch and her pity. *Did he pity himself? Was he still a man?* He didn't know whether they had taken his manhood when they had converted him. Perhaps not, testosterone was more likely to help the conversion than hinder it. Then to his surprise, he felt himself responding to her touch.

Melody stopped caressing him and snuggled closer before going to sleep again. Rick found that weariness had overtaken him and he joined her in sleep.

The next time he woke, it was around midday. Melody was not there with him. He started to panic and then willed himself to relax. She would come back. They must be the only people alive in this place.

He tested his arm and noted an improvement. The nanos were working well. The familiar presence of Mind-space was still absent and there was no sign of the uplink. For the present, he was comfortable in his own skin. The continuity of his mind stretched out to the past and he could project into the future. Melody came back, washed and in clean clothes. He noticed the well-formed breasts and her narrow waist. He liked the curve of her cheek and smiled at her.

"Feeling better, I see," she commented as she leaned over him to check his injuries. Whistling through her teeth, she nodded to herself. "You sure do heal quickly. By the way, your friends are all dead. I'm sorry. No sign of another lander yet."

"They weren't really friends," he said, still gazing at her.

"Really? Has more of your past come back?"

"Just this," he said as he reached for her. She was unresisting when he kissed her and tentative when he caressed her.

She pulled back and gaped at him. "Are you sure you want this? Can you even...you know...?"

He nodded. "Perfectly functional, I assure you."

"Yes, okay. I can see that. But what do you feel?"

"I feel...alive. Thanks to you."

"I feel like a ghost, myself. What the hey. May as well as not." Melody stripped her clothes off and lay naked beside him. Bruises and cuts patterned her arms and legs. A burn across her belly looked partially healed. Her look was intense as she reached out to touch his chin. Rick let himself be a man for the first time in ages. Most of his memories may have been gone, but what was essentially him was there, reawakening from dormancy.

Later, Melody offered him more water. He sipped it slowly while watching her face. "What's the matter?" he asked her.

"Nothing. I'm hungry. I'm going to eat. Your wounds are almost healed. Do the nanos work on the prosthetics as well?"

"I used to think so. But I recall major repairs have to be done in the workshop."

He tried moving his left arm and, although it was improving, it was a deadweight, like Mindspace. The robotics in his arm were fried.

"I'll be back soon." She tucked her hair behind her ear and headed out.

"Melody?" he called to her softly.

She paused on the threshold. "Yes?"

"Did you enjoy it?"

"Yes," she said quickly and ducked away, her cheeks pink.

He let healing sleep claim him. When he next woke, she was asleep next to him again, like a kitten, radiating warmth and trust.

Why did this girl trust him? He was part machine, programmed to kill. He didn't even trust himself. This moment with her was a respite from his life. He was healing. Uplink would resume, had to, unless he had been abandoned and given up for dead. He wanted it to be so.

He reached out and touched Melody's soft cheek and then traced his forefinger along her earlobe. When he looked at her face again, her eyes were open. Dark rings encircled her eyes and her cheeks looked drawn. Shock, he realised. The bombing and cleansing had left a mark on her.

"Why do you care about what happens to me? You should kill me," Rick said.

She grimaced and half shrugged. "You're human now. Killing you would be murder. Besides, I'm the last one left. I am the silent voice that no one will hear."

Inwardly he frowned. Everything she valued was gone and she clung to him as he was all that was left. There was no future, only the now. There was no point in arguing with her. They lay there cuddling as the early morning sun rose. He felt so warm inside when he held her. He found himself liking her smile and the way she moved. She kissed his chin quickly and sighed.

"What is it?" he whispered close to her ear.

"I wonder what we are going to do—when you're fully healed. Any sign of your uplink?"

"No. Nothing. I'm free of it. I can stay here with you."

She sighed again. "A lovely dream. If only…"

"What is to stop it?" he asked her, even though he knew. *Why did he give in to dreams? Why did he chase after a trace of hope? Because in that moment, he was who he was meant to be—a person, not a thing.*

She pulled away from him. "Mmm…I don't want to say."

He reached out and stroked along her back. "Tell me."

"They will come back for you. Maybe today, maybe tomorrow. Maybe next week."

"They would have come already if they were coming. I am sure of it." He told himself that was hope speaking, rather than admit to the lie.

She shook her head and let out a long breath through her nose. "In the past, the military have never left traces. No tech. No soldier bodies. No weapons. They'll come to collect the evidence, the troopers, the machines, and they'll remove the dead bodies of the colonists as well. It will be as if we never existed. It's just a matter of time."

He dropped his hand and looked away. There was a yawning gap of hurt inside of him. Even without Mindspace, he understood her logic, the truth as she knew it.

She shoved her arms into a shirt and pulled on her slacks. "Look, I have to find some more food. Rest, okay?"

"I'll be here waiting." He untied his leg and flexed it. It

was stiff and painful. His left arm was not one hundred per cent but he could hold a weapon, pull a trigger. He scouted around for his armour and weapons, checking before reattaching them.

He was alone in their hiding place when Mindspace flared into life. Rick jumped up as his programming began to reboot. He panicked, looking everywhere for Melody. He had to warn her before it swamped him, drowned him, buried him.

He ducked out the doorway. "Melody!" he called repeatedly. The uplink began to flash on and off as it tried to re-establish contact. He lurched around a pile of debris, over spots of his dried blood. Melody came around a corner. She saw him and began to run toward him.

"Are you okay? What is it?" she called as she ran.

Mindspace flushed his memory buffers and reasserted his programming. Panic overwhelmed him. He had no time to explain. What he was at that moment was quickly being rewritten.

"Run. Run!" he shouted in desperation. The only words he could freely form before his consciousness sank below the layers of programming and orders reasserted themselves.

Melody slowed, assessing him. Then, taking him at his word, she turned and bolted away. His eye booted up. He could see her on infrared. Orders shot through Mindspace —exterminate all colonists.

Her pace slowed and then she stopped and turned back. Staring at him with sad eyes, she whispered, "Remember me, Rick."

He heard the words with his enhanced hearing and the essence of him fought for control of his body. He unlatched his weapon from the holster on his belt. Tears fell hot and wet on his cheek as the last of him sank beneath the opaque surface of Mindspace. He sighted along the weapon, sniffed before squeezing off a shot. Melody dropped and then disappeared from infrared.

Uplink ordered a pick-up, flashing green. Rick sent an acceptance packet and headed for the rendezvous point. Mission complete. Colony cleansed.

BODILY CONTROL

Voices merged into a loud rumble as sellers hawked their wares and patrons seeking bargains snaked around stalls. Fragrant steam and smoke from the various food stalls lingered in the air as night hung at the edges, kept at bay by bright LED lights. Life flowed here and I breathed it in, enjoying my moment of freedom.

The aroma of hot broth, a mixture of chicken and pork with a hint of fish, teased my nostrils. Thick golden ramen noodles curled decoratively and small spots of oil glistened off the surface of the soup. I'd already swallowed the sliced pork and revelled in the taste of fresh pak choi leaves, softened by heat. I shovelled in the small chunks of fried tofu and then twirled the noodles around my chopsticks and shoved them into my mouth. Fresh food. So good.

Keeping my head down as I sat on the stool by the rickety counter, I flicked my gaze left and right and breathed out slowly. No one was taking any notice of me. I had time, I thought. My wrist tickled and I rubbed at it absently and I picked up the bowl, tipping the remains of the broth into my mouth. I belched and then dumped my waste container into the bin as I slid off my seat. Time to move.

Out of the stall and in the throng, a woman bumped my shoulder as she tried to pass, her hands full of shopping bags bulging with corn, celery and what looked like kale. Another person, a big man, thick set, thumped into me. "Hey, watch it!" I barked, recovering my step.

A muttered apology floated in the air, but I had to pay more attention to navigating through the bodies pressing in. I wasn't used to crowds. Not these days anyway. Turning sideways, I side stepped to weave around people. Being among them was like wearing a heavy overcoat on a too-warm day. My eyes darted around, ever vigilant. There was no doubt the crowd was increasing as work shifts changed and people came to the market.

The itch in my wrist started to burn: I needed to move. The implant was in my head but I felt it as heat in my wrist. I darted around people who plodded along or stopped to gawk. Up ahead a glowing Metro sign loomed and I aimed for it. People streamed up the stairs and out onto the streets as I aimed myself down, boots thumping on the risers. Most gazes slid over me, people with bored faces, uncon-cerned expressions, and unfocussed eyes. No one appeared to be noticing me in my dark, tight-fitting one-piece suit that was meant to be nondescript as well as protective. Must be working, I thought. My wrist burned again. I looked at it, and sighed.

Down on the concourse, the hairs on the back of my neck prickled. Eyes were on me, I was certain. Turning slightly, I checked over my shoulder before I took the esca-lator down to the platform, clump, clumping on the metal risers. Once there, I had to go with the flow of people, tight around me as they fought to reach their train. People snarled and spat at each other. *Hey! Watch it. Fuck you. Idiot. Dick wad. Excuse me!*

Even anonymous among the throng, I knew I was being followed. Had I imagined that tall, cloaked figure following me?

The burning in my wrist had lessened, and I eased out a sigh as my spine relaxed. I rubbed absently at the tingling skin as the pain faded. A train lurched to an ear-ringing, squealing halt. I joined the passengers swarming to get on. I didn't care where it was going, only that it was leaving this place.

Despite many people alighting at the station, the carriage was still full when I boarded. Clinging to the strap near a door, I stood vigilant, trying not to appear so. People stood nearby, backs turned to me, and on the seats people sat hunched over their devices, scrolling through news, watching vids. A few stared slack faced out the windows into the blur of nothing outside. For a moment it took me back to the past, of countless times I had sat in trains like this one, commuting to the office, visiting the city. The people looked the same to me. Some things change, but others don't.

A sharp jab to my thigh brought me back to the present. "Ouch!" I yelped.

Looking down, I saw a small puncture in the fabric of my trousers. A small hole in my thigh. My brain started firing questions: How did they penetrate the fabric? What is it? Did they steal my DNA or did they inject me with something? Think! Think!

I groped for my micro analyser in my back pocket and placed it over the wound. The same backs were turned toward me. The perpetrator merged into the crowded bodies, sliding through them as if oiled. I blinked and scanned my surroundings. Nada. Just some little prick who wanted a piece of me or wanted me dead. The analyser flashed a diagnostic in bright red LED. Damn it to hell: Botulinum toxin. That answered that question. Murder attempt it was. I should've guessed as they hadn't hung around to snatch me.

Flush with my breast was a pocket with my emergency kit. As the carriage rocked, I slipped out the slim carry case and selected the appropriate anti-toxin vial. A quick jab in my thigh with the injector and I relaxed as the immediate threat eased. My heart rate rocketed and it took two tries to click the injector back into its case and then slip the whole unit back into my pocket. The wound throbbed painfully. I gritted my teeth. I should've dosed myself up on analgesics too.

"Are you okay?" A voice, with a delightful French accent, sounded above me.

My head jerked up. A man had managed to slide through the bodies to stand in front of me. I tried to remain calm as I assessed my surroundings. The man was just under six foot, athletic build, longish hair, five o'clock shadow, good teeth. Very vintage George Michael, I thought with a smile. That took me back. However, I couldn't afford to get cosy with strangers on a train. It wasn't done in my youth and it definitely wasn't done now.

"I'm fine, thank you." Avoiding eye contact, I stared at the wall, pretending to look out the window, even though it was just a dark blur of subway tunnel.

"It's just that I saw that guy...He hurt you."

Damn. Don't make a bloody scene. Go away, I thought, as I levelled a fierce "go away" stare, but he smiled and gave me a Gallic shrug.

"It's nothing. I'm good." My wrist started burning anew

and I gasped in surprise. *How?* was my first thought. Then I turned my attention back to my uninvited saviour.

He leaned in closer, his breath moist against my ear. "No, it's something. Let me help you."

I righted myself and shook my head. "Don't touch me. Just go."

People looked then. I had spoken too loudly, too sharply. I didn't need the attention. Didn't want it.

My knees unlocked and I grabbed the wall as a wave of wooziness hit me. The anti-toxin didn't usually affect me that way. I looked up, mouth hanging open stupidly. The guy was looking at me still, a calm, patient expression on his face. Why hadn't he gone already?

"Steady," he said, and he grabbed my upper arm. The faintness grew worse. I tried to fight it and then a male passenger in the seat across from me slumped to the floor and a woman, one seat over, toppled sideways out of her seat. Another passenger flopped against the window. I blinked as hands, arms and bodies piled up on the ground next to my booted feet. Sucking in a breath, I stared unbelieving as everyone in the carriage crashed out into unconsciousness. I managed to gape at the French dude holding onto my arm. He was still standing. Then I saw the nostril sleeve that protected him from the gas or whatever agent had been released into the carriage.

"I'll take...care..." His voice distorted in my ears. Waves of nausea rocked me and maybe I wasn't out cold because I detected movement. My wrist burned like a hot poker pressed to it. Memories rose. Of the time before—before people I didn't know started wanting me dead or wanting a piece of me.

I had been a fifty-nine-year-old woman. Too old to be desired. Too old to matter. Past it, maybe. Not meeting society's expectations of the ideal body. No longer valued. No longer fertile. A body in decline. An opinion to be overlooked and an older person with experience and intellect that was no longer valued. I had been lucky, though, as I had had a family that cared so hadn't been a complete waste of space. I had been useful to them in some practical ways. Then, rejuvenation came into vogue. New techniques. Genetic kick start. Free trials for those who fit the criteria, which I had. With nothing to lose, I had signed up.

Had I really wanted to be young and hot or had I wanted another go at life? My fantasy had always been to have my youth over again, with all my accumulated life experience and knowledge. I can't remember what justification I gave myself—it didn't really matter now. The bad news was that rejuvenation wasn't for everyone. Only a few of us early ones were successful. The process hurt—suffocating fluids soaked in, pumped into you and vomited out of you. Months of experimentation, of treatment, and it boiled down to DNA. Rejuvenation worked on me. The jury was still out on whether it was worth it. My life, my body, hadn't been my own since they spilled me out of the vat and paraded me to the world. Now people either wanted a piece of me or wanted me dead because I represented something they wanted or hated or something they couldn't have.

Words echoed around me and brought me to consciousness. My sour-tasting tongue was stuck to the roof of my mouth. My body pressed against a hard bed and my naked skin adhered to a plastic covering beneath me. My suit was gone. My head thumped like someone with thick boots had stomped on me. Survival instincts kicked in and situational awareness grew. Dark room, medical trolley, chemical smell, pressure on my abdomen while the flesh was dull and numb. Shit! Someone was trying to do something to my body.

"Fuck! They're gone..." a deep, low voice said.

My eyes snapped open and I cringed. Pain. Blinked and swallowed, trying to grease my mouth with saliva.

"What do you mean they're gone?" another voice said. This one had a heavy accent.

"Look! No ovaries."

Something flew across the room and a metal tray smashed into the far wall. "All this risk for nothing. Put a fucken bullet in her head. She's useless."

I screamed and they jerked away from me as I sat up. "What the fuck!" I spat at them. "Where are my goddamn ovaries?"

The ultrasound wand was in a skinny, pimply guy's hand. An older, bald guy with thick shoulders stood by the ultrasound machine. "Who took my fucken ovaries?" I asked again.

They gaped at me, one blink, two. Frozen. Shocked.

I managed a breath, calmed a bit. At least these guys weren't wielding a laser knife. An ultrasound was less intrusive, a precursor to the laser knife to be sure, but not quite a threat yet. The issue was that somebody had cut me open and taken my ovaries at some stage and I didn't know when or by whom. God damn it! I couldn't remember waking up from that surgery. I had a daughter when I was younger, before rejuv. Sadly for her she inherited my longevity genes and she hated me for it. Her life was as fucked up as mine. The curse, she called it. She wasn't wrong.

I detected a presence behind me. "You don't know?" said a familiar voice. The French guy came up to the trolley and stepped into view. "That's incredible. Unbelievable even."

"Unlikely," the older guy said. "She probably sold them. She's rolling in money." He reached down to his belt, pulled out a gun.

"Yeah, greedy bitch," said the other skinny, pimply dude, waving the ultrasound wand.

"I'm not greedy. Bastards! Do you know how many times I've been abducted? How many times someone has tried to take a piece of me or kill me?"

The French guy gave me another Gallic shrug, a sort of *I don't care but I'm happy to listen* expression. "No. How many?"

"I don't know. Too many to count. And no one told me that I'd lost my ovaries." I should have felt grief at the loss and the violation but didn't. I was strangely dead to all that stuff. I was one hundred and twenty years old. I wasn't going to use what was left of my eggs.

"How is this possible?" Frenchie asked me, suddenly interested.

I shook my head, not quite believing my ears. That made my head throb so I stopped the movement. "You abducted me in a public place, gassed everyone in that carriage despite my protections, to get to me? That's how."

He scoffed. "Protections? What protections? You were alone, vulnerable. There are cameras everywhere, facial recognition. Easy to hack. We followed you. You have no protection. You're just a little idiot!" He pronounced the last without the "t".

Technically, the suit was protection. That was gone. They must have cut it off. I also had an analyser, back-up anti-toxins and wound kits that I took with me when I was out. They were with my suit, it seemed. The heat in my wrist increased, if such a thing was possible. Luckily endorphins kicked in and dulled the pain.

"I do have other protections. You'd better leave while you still can," I said in a bored voice and rubbed my wrist. I wasn't very insistent.

"Your robot bodyguard can't find you here. We researched its capabilities. We took countermeasures."

I looked at my wrist. The sensor in my brain was telling my wrist to hurt. That told me that my protection was nearby.

They had abducted me and wanted to harm me. The guy with the gun glared as if still tossing up whether to end me right then. The French guy frowned at me and cocked his head and watched me trying to soothe away the heat.

The skinny guy with the ultrasound wand tossed it back into the holder. "It isn't right. Why should the rich be the ones to be fertile? Why should they inherit the Earth? Why should they have extended life and youthful bodies?"

"I'm not rich, okay!" I shouted back at him. This wasn't my fault. "Rejuvenation was an experiment when I volunteered."

"You help them. You represent them," the guy with the gun growled out.

I watched the gun and then looked him hard in the eye. "I don't. Not in the way you think."

The French guy touched my hand. I met his gaze. "You sold yourself to the corporates. They have patented everything. They won't share so we must take."

I let out a breath. "My DNA was claimed by the genealogical site I used to do family history back in the day. Before I undertook rejuvenation treatment. Back when DNA wasn't worth anything. When they discovered I had a gene that was switched on during the rejuv process, that tied up the courts while the corporates fought over ownership. When the court case concluded, I had to give them ownership of my post rejuv DNA profile or they'd bankrupt me. Going in, I didn't know the treatment would work. I didn't know it would make me look so young. Let me live this long. They didn't know. No one did." I sucked in a breath. "I didn't have a say. It was a goddam unforeseen side effect!"

"You disgust me," said the medical guy, shoving the ultrasound machine so it crashed into the wall. "You keep signing up to corporates. Sponsorships, what have you. Complicit. That's what you are."

I moved my head slowly to meet his eye. "Yes. I have to. I can't afford round the clock protection, a safe place to live. Every ten years I need to sign up to a new contract. They pay me a little but they own me. They own this body and every cell in it. Even when I die, if I die, they will own it then too."

The gun rose, aimed at me. "You live in luxury, have every need met while the rest of us fight to live and are destined to die out."

"Hey, don't," said the French guy. "There's more to this. Let her speak."

Accepting the invitation, I responded. "If you think I wanted to live like this, you're crazy. I have no life. I was out on the street less than half an hour and was attacked twice."

"You did it for money. Sold yourself." The older guy's voice was quiet but firm.

"If that's what you think, I can't change your mind. You should leave, by the way." My wrist was so hot I thought the skin would singe.

"Why should we leave? No one followed us here. We took precautions."

I tilted my head, gauging how sincerely I wanted to save the French guy. If they didn't leave, they were all going to die or be seriously broken.

"What precautions? Did you destroy my bodyguard?"

The French guy shook his head.

"Well, you didn't take enough precautions."

The big guy folded his arms and glared. "We took plenty. You can't be found down here."

"Right. Don't listen to me. What do I know?"

"What do you do with the money you do get?" the French guy asked.

"Charity. Fertility programs mostly." I grasped my wrist and winced. "It's not like I can enjoy it. Ow!"

"What is it?" The French guy moved closer, thankfully blocking the aim of the gunman. "Why are you in pain?"

"It's a proximity alert. It's too late. AIDSU is coming."

The ground vibrated. They braced, fear on their features. The skinny guy took a step forward and then back, uncertain where to go. The far wall shook; a crack started from floor to ceiling. The French guy looked up and jumped back.

The older guy yelled, "Move out of the way! I can kill her."

The French guy met my gaze and then turned to the others and shrugged. "Why? How will that help us now?"

A massive force punctured a hole in the far wall. Wood, bricks and sheeting blew out. I covered my head, then peered into the pale light streaming in through the haze of debris. The three men were no longer standing. Their groans peppered the sound of falling masonry as they struggled to stand.

"I suggest you run," I said to my captors.

They just started to yell, climbed to their feet and

waved their arms and threw things. I sat on the trolley, folded my legs and closed my eyes, with my hands over my head. I didn't like this part. I didn't want to see.

AIDSU, my Artificial Intelligence Driven Support Unit, was built like a man but was as solid as a tank. He could withstand just about anything thrown at him. He was tasked with looking after me. He was a dead bore most of the time. The subway dulled the signal, making me hard to pinpoint. That's why I went down there to keep my distance after I gave him the slip when my appointment with my current contract holder ended.

A wet thud sounded. I squeezed my eyes shut. Pity I couldn't block out the smell of blood and ripped intestines. I didn't like gore in the flesh. I preferred artificial murder in my media feed. I wished my hearing wasn't so acute. A yell and another swoosh of air and a flick of hot liquid hit my cheek. A sound something like a plastic bag breaking and a dull thump indicated the last abductor had been dealt with.

"Reggie?" AIDSU said in his smoothly modulated male voice. I had tried programming him with my favourite actors' voices, but given they were all dead it became morbid so I changed it back to his native voice. "Reggie, are you unharmed?"

He was scanning me so would find out himself. "Yes. I think so." I didn't feel great. "What does your scanner say?"

"You have residual toxins in your blood. Your stomach recently emptied and I see you have an oxygen deprivation headache. You should administer some analgesics before I return you to base."

He walked around the room and then went back out through the hole he had made. I groaned when he walked back with a slim, human-shaped bag in tow. "Not the skin," I complained.

"Yes, the skin. Flowers of argument are unnecessary by reason of protection." He bent to pick up his cloak. He thought the cloak hid him well but I thought it made him look like an oversized Dracula. People looked at him in the cloak or without.

I frowned at him. "Have you been playing around with your literary program? Or are you damaged?"

"I am not damaged. Please get in the skin."

I sighed. Wiped at the blood on my cheek and slipped off the medical trolley. "Can you sedate me? You know I hate that thing." It was like a body bag of old, but more. It shielded me, hid me as well providing life support. It was claustrophobic as all hell. It was like being in a coffin.

I lay down in it and looked up at AIDSU. He had black skin and a yellow glow instead of whites to his eyes. Otherwise he wasn't bad to look at in an artificial kind of way.

He bent down to set the skin to seal, spraying sedative in my face as he did so. I so hate skin travel, I thought as I shut my eyes.

I woke up in my own bed, a tad hungover. I had been dreaming about ramen, then realised it was a memory. That meal had tasted so good. The atmosphere at the market had connected me to life in a way that living here in the bunker never did. We were underground: artificial light, stale air, a one-bedroom-sized construction, with small living area and a galley kitchen.

No sound other than AIDSU, who seemed to be cooking. No life other than my own.

I stepped into the shower, letting the warmth seep into my skin and clean away the street dirt and the blood. I leaned on the shower wall, letting a wave of nausea and fear wash over me. Those people were dead because of me. It didn't matter that they might have killed me. More likely they would have ransomed me to the corporation that owned my body at the moment. The corporation owned AIDSU too but he didn't seem to mind—it was all he knew.

After washing and drying my hair and putting another overall on, I walked out to the common area. The big wall screen showed a rain forest with mist and rain. I lifted my mouth in a half smile. AIDSU was trying to comfort me. He always did when I escaped from him. "What's for dinner?" I asked and flumped down on the easy chair.

"Coq au vin, garlic mashed potatoes and young beans," he replied, turning around. I saw he was wearing an apron and blinked. That was new. "Before you ask, I have flavoured the escape route with my internal gifts and changed all the security pops so you can't be out unescorted again."

I blinked and burst out laughing. "Flavoured the escape route? Am I to lick my way out next time?"

AIDSU turned back to stirring the pot. "I will recalibrate my dialogue program. You cannot lick your way out of here."

"That's good news, I suppose. What did the corporates say when you reported my escape?"

"You are on your third warning. They said don't do it again or they will evoke Clause Ten penalties."

"Oh right. They will take back some of the paltry sum they pay me that I can't spend."

I sat there and stared at nothing. It didn't pay to dwell on life. I had had one once until vanity ruined it all. I had one family connection alive, my daughter. I didn't know where she was and, even after all this time, if she would even speak to me if we met. I was sure she could find me, contact me, just like I could her. What was the point? It was my fault. I started it because I wanted to have a hot and sexy and relevant body.

While dinner baked in the oven, AIDSU sat across from me, setting up the chess board. I wasn't in the mood. We played to pass the time. He always won. "What took you so long to find me this time?"

AIDSU put down the black queen and placed it on the board, then reached for the king. "You went underground, which interferes with the tracker."

"Before that, I felt you near."

"You were enjoying yourself. My senses indicated intense physical pleasure."

"You felt pity?"

"I do not feel."

"I went underground because I felt you coming. But that wouldn't stop you normally. Well, not for long."

He peered up at me and then reached for the bishops. "They used something like the skin to transport you along the subway tunnel. It blanked the tracker until I could recalibrate."

"Oh?" I said, vaguely, thinking they had had intel then and come prepared. "And then?"

"That lab was underground and it took a while to triangulate your position and choose the best place to enter."

I nodded and rubbed at my chin. "Your timing wasn't bad this time."

He bowed his head. "Thankfulness rises up."

I blinked. "I thought you fixed that AI bullshit you're spouting."

He cocked his head. "I am recalibrating. It will take a few hours."

AIDSU started arranging the white pieces even though I wasn't interested in playing. He would play by himself if I refused and attribute the loss to me. "Why did you run off, Reggie? I thought you liked it here."

I scoffed. "Like it here!" I gestured to our bunker.

"You are protected. That is paramount. That is my mission. I thought you wanted that too."

I glared at him and then felt sorry for him. He was stuck here with me because that was his programming. He was corporate owned just like me. "Sometimes I've got to have a little bit of bodily control. You know? That's what living is all about. I need to get out—to experience life, the world."

"I do not understand. You are safe here. No one touches your body unless you ask them to."

I nodded and a tear slid down my cheek. He was the only other body that coexisted with me. Sometimes he held me when I cried, read to me when I was sad, sang to me until I screamed for him to stop.

It was more than that, I thought. Out there people wanted a piece of me or wanted me and what I stood for erased. In my darker moments, I thought they were right. In my lighter moments, I just wanted to be up there, the air shifting the strands of my hair, the smell of cooking food on the breeze, the bodily knowledge that I was surrounded by people, by life, maybe laughter. "I know, AIDSU."

There was no point in trying to explain to him. He wasn't even a him really. I just made him into one because that suited me. I sat back and closed my eyes, knowing that AIDSU would wait an hour, a day even for me to make the next move: play, eat or sleep or try to escape when we had to go somewhere.

I let my mind wander, seeking to understand when I had lost control of my body. I knew the how and I knew the why but when was the question. Was it after I reached age thirty? Or when I turned forty-five? Maybe it was fifty-five when reality sank in, when I realised I was old. I knew by that time I no longer earned the big salary, I was no longer relevant. What was important then was the young, the smartly dressed, the fit and sexy, who had brains and jobs and high disposable incomes. It was not their fault though. They were part of the machine that grinds us all to dust. Except, I didn't fall into dust. I was still ground down though. The corporates owned me. They didn't own my mind. It's the only thing I had. No bodily control.

"Knight to bishop two," I said, giving in.

If AIDSU had been human, he might have clapped with excitement. He swiftly made his move and then watched me like a cat, waiting for my next move, while my stomach growled as we waited for dinner.

We played until I tipped my king over, losing again. AIDSU brought my dinner over. It was delicious, chicken, wine and mushrooms, and he watched me as I ate, using his senses to see if I really liked it. It tasted divine and I let it show.

I never beat him at chess because I saved all my strategies to get away, to trick him, put him out of action so I could exercise a little bodily control.

Sometimes, he let me.

BE STILL MY BEATING CLOCKWORK HEART

Miss Elizabeth McGrath stepped down from the carriage with the assistance of the coachman, who offered his hand as she navigated the step and let his fingers linger too long on her elbow. Pretending not to notice, Elizabeth nodded politely and corrected the angle of her plain black bonnet and smoothed out the wrinkles in the skirt of her silk mourning dress. It did not do to meet one's relations looking blousy and unkempt. Her two travelling chests thumped as they were dropped on the ground.

Staring at the rundown terrace house, she hid her chagrin. No one had come out to meet her. Elizabeth gathered up her skirts and skittered along the short path to lift the door knocker. Her luggage was dumped behind her on the weed-filled path as she knocked. Her hat boxes and small travelling case were stacked upon her two chests. With a tilt of her head, along with a half penny, she bestowed her thanks on the porter, and turned to meet the old woman who opened the door.

The woman's cap was greyish and her brown dress drab. "Yes?" the old woman said with very little interest.

"My name is Miss Elizabeth McGrath." She stepped to the side so the servant would see her trunks. "I'm here for a visit with my Aunt Sylvester-Smythe and Aunt Beatrice. I sent a letter last week."

"Wait a moment, Miss." The servant made to shut the door.

Elizabeth put out a gloved hand. "Please, I'd rather not stand on the porch with all the world to see me from the street."

After a clash of glares, the servant relented and let her into the hallway. A tattered carpet led further into the house.

"Is there a manservant who can bring in my chests?"

Elizabeth was not keen to leave them on the stoop. A breeze entered the house through the open door and stirred up the dust in the hall. Not a good thing. She sneezed into her lace kerchief and wished herself miles away.

The old woman lumbered painfully down the hall, obviously favouring her right leg. She paused before bellowing out "Angus!" into the house's nether regions. With a decided frown between her brows, the old servant turned, grasped the banister and hauled herself up the stairs, one riser at a time. It was painful to watch. What kind of house was she visiting? That woman should have been pensioned off, not made to continue on with a lame leg.

Elizabeth fidgeted, hating the fact she had to stay with relatives whom she had never met before and who, by all accounts, had never taken an interest in her. But promises were promises and not cabbages, as her old nurse used to say.

Before long, a large old man, with tuffs of grey hair sticking up from his bald head and hands like plates, lurched up the hallway. Undaunted, Elizabeth drew herself up to her five foot one inch.

"Good day. Would you be so kind as to bring my trunks inside the house? I'm not quite sure where I'll be sleeping. That heavy, carved one can stay downstairs, if you like."

Angus lifted his head, grunted and barrelled past her. Elizabeth had no recourse but to step further inside. Here she caught sight of her reflection in the hallstand mirror. *Oh dear!* She looked dishevelled. Hurriedly releasing her blonde ringlets from the constraints of her bonnet, she rubbed some colour into her cheeks. They were old aunts but she wanted to make a good impression, despite their obliviousness to her visit.

Angus dumped the first trunk in the hallway, grunting and muttering. This he slid, pushing up the threadbare carpet. Then he went for the next, dragging the heavy one inside and leaving it under the stairs, jaw clenched and muscles bunching as he pushed and shoved it out of the way. He went out again for the rest of her things—a carpet bag and two bandboxes—and dropped them noisily onto the trunk. He jerked his chin at her and shuffled past to return from whence he came. Not very promising at all. It looked like she was preparing to leave rather than arrive. Angus slouched away, leaking the smell of chimney smoke and gin in his wake. Before long, the old female servant returned. "My mistresses will see you now. This way."

Elizabeth draped the ribbons of her bonnet over her arm and followed the servant, who worked her way slowly up the stairs. This gave her time to gather her dignity along with her skirts.

The old woman threw the door open and then limped

away, leaving Elizabeth to walk in unannounced. The smell of must and vinegar met her as soon as she entered. Elizabeth had smelt worse in her time, visiting local hovels to attend the poor and the sick. She nudged the door further, then took a few steps inside. The drawn curtains made the room gloomy. In the shadows, two stooped forms hunched over as they sat in easy chairs upholstered in faded and ragged chintz.

"I beg your pardon. I'm Elizabeth McGrath; my father was your brother, Rupert McGrath."

"Shut the door. We'll catch our death," cackled one.

"The draft, girl. The draft," whined the other.

Elizabeth tilted her head and turned to close the door. The room was rather warm. A few embers glowed in the fireplace and the old aunts appeared to be swathed in quilts.

"I'm sorry to intrude. But were you expecting me? You did receive my letter?"

"She's going to be a problem. Always talking, talking," said the younger of the aunts, Beatrice.

"Of course we received your letter and the one from your father as well. Can't be bothered with letters." This was Aunt Sylvester-Smythe.

"Useful for starting the fire," commented Beatrice and then she honked like a goose.

Elizabeth chewed her lip. Her father had been angry when they hadn't responded to his letter and grumbled about their long memories and straight-laced prejudices.

"Were you expecting me for a visit? I wrote to you from Uncle Edwin McGrath's. He sends greetings, by the way."

Aunt Sylvester-Smythe nodded with a toothless grin.

"You're here now, aren't you? I suppose we'll have to

put up with you," Aunt Beatrice said, before taking out a rag and blowing her nose noisily on it.

"That's very kind of you. I hope I'm not putting you out. Father wanted me to visit all my relations. He left me a list, you see."

"It's all very well for him to leave a list. Not consulted us about it, has he?" the older aunt replied.

Elizabeth understood that it had been the purport of her father's letter, but held her peace.

"Doesn't do to speak ill of the dead," Beatrice said and began to pick at her nose.

"Well, if Edwin let you stay, I suppose we can. He is rather an odd creature. I do not know how you bore his company." This was the older sister, Aunt Silvester-Smythe.

The other aunt grunted with what sounded like agreement. What strange creatures these two were and so opposite to her scholarly and inventive father. He had been such a brilliant man. Elizabeth was hard-pressed to see how they were siblings. It made her feel a tad melancholy.

Elizabeth looked away, taking in the slovenly room, the cobwebs hanging from the cornices, the layer of soot on everything and the general smell of the place, which she thought centred on the aunts. They were old, she supposed, but she had never been exposed to incontinence before.

"Call out to Molly will you? She can show you where you can sleep. I hope you brought your woollens because it's cold up there in the attics," the elder aunt advised.

"No fireplaces up there," Beatrice chimed in.

Elizabeth dropped a curtsy. "You are very kind to offer me shelter. I shall go and freshen up. What time do you dine?"

Aunt Beatrice cackled, nearly tipping from her chair. "Dine? You are a ripe one, aren't you?"

Elizabeth furrowed her brow. Surely the old women ate.

"Ask Molly," Aunt Silvester-Smythe said with a determined sneer. "She will inform you of our timetable."

Elizabeth thanked her aunts again and returned to the landing. She leaned on the door and sighed. God in heaven, how was she to last the requisite six weeks with those old hags? Oh how she wished she had not promised her father so faithfully that she would, wished she had not vowed on the life he had saved all those years ago.

The servant, Molly, was nowhere to be seen so she descended the stairs and went in search of her. She found Molly with her holey-gloved hand wrapped around a chipped cup, sipping a drink. Opposite was Angus, slurping away at a tankard.

"Excuse me, Molly. My aunts told me to find out where I'll be sleeping and what time dinner will be."

Molly tied on a stained apron. "Up in the attic, first door on the left. Mind yer head, there's a low beam on the stair. I'll call yer when dinner's ready."

"Thank you." She turned to leave.

"We don't eat fancy here." She reached for a large mixing bowl. "My mistresses 'ave plain taste."

"I'm sure whatever you serve will be wholesome."

Standing at the door to her room, she found it difficult to hold back the tears. It was a filthy hovel, with a lumpy mattress on top of an antique wooden frame. A small window let in cold light, mirroring the despair in her heart. If the household thought the condition of the room fit for a visiting relative, she had no expectations of her dinner beyond a bowl of thin gruel. It was the opposite of her old life on a small country estate in Kent, with her light-filled room overlooking a small stand of oaks and the old village church. A house filled with learning and love.

She wiped at the tears on her cheeks and stared at them on the ends of her fingers. There was no point in being maudlin. This was her life now and she better step up to it quick like.

Angus made a song and dance about bringing up her luggage. Thankfully, she asked for the heaviest one to remain downstairs. He wobbled on the stairs as he returned for the rest and she worried he was too intoxicated to manage. However, he did and complained loudly about it.

After changing out of her travelling clothes, she put on an old house dress so she could clean the chamber. As she cleaned out the accumulated muck, she thought about alternative arrangements for accommodation. It was possible to take a room in a boarding house instead, but as a woman alone in the town, there was her reputation to worry about. Besides, she had promised her father before he died that she would stay with each of her relatives according to the list, for the specified amount of time. And there was no going back on that promise. Since she was a young girl, following her father's exact instructions had been what kept her alive.

A lifetime of such exactitude was hard to overthrow, no matter how miserable she was feeling. Her home had been entailed to a cousin, the son of her father's next brother, who had died six months before her own father. Her income, while modest, would keep her well enough. It did not extend to expensive lodgings, the hiring of a maid, or luxury travel.

Down in the kitchen, Molly sniffed when Elizabeth sought a bucket of hot water and a scrubbing brush and cleaning rags. "That room's clean enough."

"No insult intended, Molly. I'm afraid I'm rather fastidious. Cleaning helps me settle in."

The old servant was not mollified by Elizabeth's attempt to spare her feelings. She grunted and sniffed when bringing them.

As Elizabeth carried the heavy bucket up the stairs, she thought the servant was old and incapable of cleaning a large old house. It wasn't Molly's fault. She needed help. Obviously, the old aunts would not pay for additional servants. Elizabeth knew what money they had so it was not as if they could not afford it.

The small window lifted after no small amount of tugging, which helped air the room. After dusting and sweeping for cobwebs, she started on the floor. Her muscles ached as she mopped up the last dregs, the water now black. Her heart beat like the innards of a clock.

When she returned the bucket, she retrieved her sheets, airing them in front of the kitchen range. Once the bed was made up, Elizabeth fashioned one of her shawls as a curtain for the window.

Shaking her head, she took in the room. At least this wasn't where she would live the rest of her life. Her six-week visit to her youngest uncle had been pleasant enough. Although she could not say she knew him any better for it. He alluded to the fact that he and her father had not got on. Something vague about a squabble regarding money and love. Elizabeth had never uncovered the truth of the matter. Her uncle barely spoke more than two words together—a silent and brooding man.

Her travelling trunk remained to be unpacked. She ferreted around in her reticule to look at the letter her father had written. It comforted her to see his words and to know that he had thought so well of her, even at the end of his life.

Rather than go downstairs to beg for more hot water,

Elizabeth poured some cold water from the jug into the washing bowl and stripped down to her petticoat to wash. The key on its silver chain bounced against her chest. The old house dress she had worn while cleaning was bunched into a ball for laundry later. She expected there was no laundry maid so she would do it herself in the morning. Perhaps Molly might have thawed by then, but she doubted it.

SUPPER WAS AS SHE FEARED. The old women took theirs in their beds and did not impart any apologies for not joining her. While her meal did not consist of gruel, it was a thin barley soup and a hunk of stale bread, eaten in her room. She felt most unwelcome and rather sad. It was times like these she missed her father most. He had always talked to her and had always been considerate of her needs, if somewhat over protective.

The parlour where she had greeted her relatives smelt so bad she could not think to eat in there and the small library downstairs was not clean. Elizabeth would see to that in the morning. Surely her aunts would not mind if she used it for her own pursuits. They did not come downstairs at all. The thought of discovering hidden treasures in her deceased uncle's small library brought a smile to her face. As she lay down to sleep, she realised she had something worthwhile to do the next day.

THE AUNTS FOUND the suggestion that she clean and attend to the library downstairs as a sign that she could be useful after all. After gruel for breakfast, which Elizabeth fought to keep down, she set to the task. Furniture had been stacked up haphazardly and Angus was employed in rearranging or removing it for storage elsewhere. The curtains were brought down in a shower of dust and taken out the back to be beaten and cleaned. Her uncle's collection of books was soon revealed and she set about dusting them. Her finger slid along the spines, noting the classics and a few histories. There was a book with no markings on the spine and she pulled it out. A few photographs fell to the floor. She picked them up and gasped. Two naked ladies were kissing in one. She slipped it behind the other and nearly choked when she realised what the man and the woman were doing. The book held more of these photos in which she became deeply engrossed.

While she studied them, she wondered about where they came from and realised they were not meant for general consumption. Surely they were wicked pictures, but how could something so enthralling be wicked? Was she now wicked for gazing at them?

A knock at the front door interrupted her. The book fell from her hand, scattering the photographs onto the carpet. Molly mumbled a few words and then flung the door open. "In here."

Face aflame, Elizabeth desperately swept the photographs between the leaves of the book and shoved it back onto the shelf.

A man walked through the door, bowler hat in his hand. Of medium height, his dark hair was unfashionably long, curling to his collar, and he had a very restrained moustache gracing his upper lip. His eyes were a warm brown and there was a gleam in his eye as he beheld her. He had a pleasant face, even though he had no smile. He paused on the threshold.

Elizabeth quickly ripped off her soot-covered apron and attempted to rub dirt off her hands and kick the old coals back into the fire place.

He gazed at her for a few breaths.

Tilting her head to the side, she locked gazes with Molly who still hovered by the door. "Thank you, Molly. That will be all."

The sound of her voice prompted the stranger to speak. He glanced over his shoulder at the departing servant and then faced her again. With a polite nod of his head, he said, "Forgive the intrusion. Do you happen to be Miss McGrath?"

Elizabeth tossed the soiled apron into the coal bucket. "I am, sir." Her face was still heated and her belly felt strange and curdled. "One of them at least."

"My name is Inspector Higgins."

"As in a police inspector?" Guilt over seeing those photographs made her blush. Surely he could not know. *Of course not!*

"Yes. I am here on official business. Pray take a seat."

"What?" Her heart thumped—too much excitement for one day. "What has happened?"

"I'm sorry to say, I have some sad news."

Elizabeth sucked in a breath and faintness crawled up her calves and invaded her knees. She must have started to swoon because his strong hand grasped her elbow and guided her to a seat.

"Truly?" she asked breathily, quite overwhelmed. "I have no notion of how you could have sad news for me." The only person close to her heart was already dead. "Surely, there is some mistake."

After asking her permission, Inspector Higgins sat opposite her. "I believe you were recently in Kent, staying with your uncle, Mr Edwin McGrath."

Elizabeth's heart ticked double time. She nodded and then twisted her fingers in her skirts. "Yes. Why, what has happened?"

"I'm afraid he has passed away."

"What? But I was just there…" She swallowed once, gathering up her good manners. "I'm so sorry to hear that. I did not know him well as he was rather reclusive. I had no notion that he was ill. He never mentioned it and I…well, I saw no sign of it."

Inspector Higgins shook his head, his brown eyes looking rather sad. "He did not die of an illness, Miss McGrath."

"An accident?" Elizabeth was surprised. The old man did not take exercise, or hunt or travel.

"I'm afraid not."

Elizabeth frowned as she puzzled it out. "I am afraid I do not understand you."

His dark brown gaze held hers. "He was murdered."

Elizabeth recoiled. "What? When?"

Inspector Higgins stood up and walked to the door and turned around. "Murdered, but I dare not go into details, Miss McGrath. It was brutal and bloody. We think the event took place the day you left, possibly a few hours before your departure."

Elizabeth launched out of her seat. "Heaven forbid!" Grasping her kerchief, she buried her face. "How horrible!" she said after a minute. "Before I left? No, not possible. I didn't see or hear anything."

"Yes, that is what we think at this stage."

"Oh, the poor, poor man. Is there anything I can do?" Her hands twisted together in her lap.

"I have a few questions for you, if you would be so kind." He gestured to the seat she had been sitting in.

"Certainly, but pray excuse me one moment."

Elizabeth left the room and staggered down the hallway. Uncle murdered? It was so difficult to believe. The same day? Their goodbyes had been said the night before as she was to leave early in the morning. She found the servant in the kitchen. "Oh Molly, could you please bring the policeman some tea and let my aunts know that there is some terrible news regarding their brother."

Molly sniffed. "The kettle is boiling already."

"Thank you." Elizabeth took a few moments to compose herself and to check her appearance in the hall mirror. There was a smudge of soot on her nose. She really wasn't dressed for receiving visitors.

Feeling more composed, Elizabeth poured the tea and handed the cup to Inspector Higgins. He watched her closely and her cheeks burned. "Thank you, Miss McGrath."

"You are welcome, sir. I am sorry to receive you like this. I've only just arrived and my aunts are not well and do not entertain visitors regularly. You caught me in the act of making this room habitable."

His gaze flicked about the room and he nodded. "A reasonable library. Do you enjoy reading?" He shook his head. "Forgive me. That was impertinent."

Elizabeth warmed to the man, as she lowered her head, feeling shy all of a sudden.

"May I meet your aunts? I have a few questions for them as well."

"I will certainly seek to introduce you, Mr Higgins."

He smiled at her, his brown eyes kind, the skin around them crinkling with a smile. She found herself responding to him, liking him.

Her questioning had been a gentle affair, his voice always soft and carefully probing. Elizabeth appreciated his consideration. It was not what she expected from a policeman. She gave him a simple recount of her visit and the morning she left. She related what she had seen and heard on that morning and on her journey. He was also interested in the days preceding and whether her uncle had any enemies. She confessed she knew of none, except the fact that apparently her father (who was also deceased) had not got on well with him.

Molly knocked on the door. "If you will come this way," she said. The inspector rose and followed her upstairs to meet the aunts.

A haze of depression hung over Elizabeth as she remained behind in the library. It was so disagreeable having such relations. What would he think of them? Would that cloud his judgement of her? What a ninnyhammer. While the policeman-detective was rather handsome and kind, he would not be interested in her. She, of course, should not be interested in him. A lady did not associate with the working classes. She waited anxiously, certain he would stop to speak to her before he left.

He came back to the library and asked if she would show him her things. He was particularly interested in her clothes. She took him upstairs to her attic room and let him look through her clothes and other belongings. She blushed when he riffled through her petticoats and underthings. He examined her aprons and gowns closely, particularly the hems. Some had not been washed and she felt humbled as he examined each one and then put them back carefully.

They returned to the library door. "Thank you for your time today, Miss McGrath. I'm sorry for the intrusion but we must be thorough in our investigation." He reached out and shook her hand. Her skin tingled in response, her breath catching in her throat. "Please let me know if there is anything I can do for you during your stay."

Nervously, she glanced at him and saw straight away the sympathy there in his look. He did not despise her for her aunts: he pitied her. Normally such feelings would make her angry, but from him they were warm and welcome.

"Thank you, sir. I am here for another five weeks or so. I'm sure I will become acquainted with this part of town."

"Then if you will permit me, I will call in now and again to keep you abreast of the investigation."

Her eyes widened. "That would be most welcome. Thank you."

To her delight the inspector called again not two days later. He joined her in the little library and asked her how she did.

Elizabeth offered him tea, which he declined.

"There are some pleasant walks about. If you are lucky you will see a range of birds in the woods. I have spied a number of rare ones."

"Why thank you. I should like to include some exercise in my daily routine. I am afraid I do not know a lot about birds but I would be pleased to learn."

That comment brought a shine to his eyes and a smile to his face.

"Do you have some paper handy?"

She went to the shelf, careful not to disturb the book where the photos were kept, and brought out some paper and a pen and ink. He spent the rest of the visit drawing her maps of the walks and pointing out where the old Roman villa and the remains of the old castle were to be found. He also told her about the Roman-built bridge that was still in use.

As he stood to take his leave, she rubbed her palms against her skirts. It had been such an enjoyable visit. He was such easy company. "You are very considerate to spend time with me, sir. I am very grateful. I hope your investigations are progressing."

"Not that well. We're still seeking to question everyone who had been to your uncle's house, which includes trades-men, and local farmers who dropped off goods."

"That does sound rather tedious. I hope you find an answer soon. Poor Uncle Edwin."

"Yes. It can be time consuming. Was there anyone in particular you remember in those last few days?"

She lowered her gaze as she had been studying his face. "No. Nothing out of the ordinary. I'm so sorry."

He stood up and checked his fob watch. "Forgive me. I've taken up too much of your time."

She stood also to show him to the door. "Thank you for your visit and the map."

The front door was open. He picked up his hat from the hall stand and paused on the threshold. "If you will permit me to visit again."

"Most certainly. I am most anxious to hear of your progress."

With a bow of the head, he was gone. Elizabeth watched him walk down the short path to the street. He had rather broad shoulders in that tweed coat of his.

A FEW WEEKS PASSED. Elizabeth, dressed in her black silk, took walks to the shops to buy supplies and small treats for her aunts. Every luncheon she braved the stench to sit with them, although the conversation was sporadic and not very entertaining.

"You look like your mother," said Aunt Sylvester-Smythe sharply.

"She has Rupert's big feet and nose," added Beatrice.

Elizabeth passed a finger along her unremarkable straight nose. Beatrice had a wicked tongue. No wonder she never married.

"I will be leaving in a week or two. I'm to travel to cousin Clarence, in Brighton."

"That old coot. You will not be welcome there. The old miser."

Elizabeth smiled. Following her father's wishes was becoming more difficult as the days dragged on. The only highlight of this visit was that the nice inspector called once or twice a week to bring her news on the investigation into her uncle's death. Her heart whispered that he came to see her, rather than doing his duty, for they talked of books, and walks in parks and bird watching, which was his particular passion. There had not been any further news on who had killed her uncle or why.

Later that night, she prepared for bed. Checking the list her father had left her, she ran through the instructions. She had to wind her heart four times every night before bed. He had invented the clockwork device for her when a fever had weakened her heart and the doctor had predicted she would die. He would have none of that. He had failed to save her mother from death so he had done his utmost to save their child. She climbed into bed with socks on and a shawl about her shoulders. The room was so cold she could see her breath misting.

The sound of ticking sent her off to sleep. *Tick. Tick. Tick. Tick.* One more day, two more days, three...*tick tock. Tick tock.*

Another luncheon—a sparse sandwich of dripping and cheese. Elizabeth was sure she was losing weight, as she was hungry so much of the time. She had no hope of becoming one of those well-rounded females in the wicked photographs. While she had an ample bosom, her behind was not very notable at all.

"Why did your father send you to us?" Beatrice asked before hacking into a rag.

Elizabeth tried not to flinch. "He did not say. He only asked that I would do him this last favour."

"Makes no sense to me," ventured the older aunt. "We did not take to your mother at all."

Elizabeth put down her cup and swallowed a lump of dry bread. "You did not like my mother?"

"No, we did not," added Beatrice. "Butcher's daughter. Had money and beauty. No breeding."

"Not a respectable lady to be sure," finished Aunt Sylvester-Smythe.

Elizabeth gaped at them. She had no notion of her mother's history. A common butcher's daughter?

"Refused to visit her. All of us." Beatrice grinned evilly.

The elder aunt turned to her sister. "Never even sent

condolences when she died. Good riddance, we all thought."

"That is correct. We never acknowledged her. Beneath us in every way. No manners to speak of, no deportment nor accomplishments." Beatrice shoved a piece of bread in her mouth and chewed with her mouth open, showing jagged brown teeth.

Elizabeth tried to breathe through her mental confusion. Her mother embroidered beautifully and some of the paintings she had in storage were watercolours her mother had painted. They were very fine indeed. Hadn't she gone to an expensive finishing school?

Yet, if her mother was lowborn as they said, no wonder her relatives were so unfeeling toward her. Why on earth would her father put her through that? Make her endure their prejudice and dislike?

"It must be very trying for you to have me visit with you."

"Pfft. You are most annoying when you whine," countered Aunt Beatrice.

"I did not know that I did whine. Forgive my impertinence." She stood up from the table, no longer able to eat. "I thank you for your hospitality." With her skirts in her hand, she moved to the door. "Pray excuse me."

Elizabeth left the room to take refuge in her own. She replayed the last conversation with her father. How ardent he had been about those who she was to visit and that she should never waver from her task. It was of the utmost importance to him. Now she saw he had ignored them in life but not in death. She was to be the reminder of his past misdeeds and their patent dislike of her mother. Did he have no inkling how hard that would be for her? What a soul-destroying experience? She put her hand on her heart.

She owed her life to her father, but a small voice inside said he asked too much.

~

"I BELIEVE you will be leaving shortly to travel to Brighton." Inspector Higgins sat on the sofa in the little library.

"Yes, tomorrow." Her voice was forlorn as Elizabeth handed him a cup of tea.

"So far away." His fingers brushed hers when he took the cup. Her gaze flicked to his face and her eyes widening involuntarily at the contact. A small tremor of delight.

It took a few moments for her to speak. "Yes." She turned her attention back to the tray. "Yes, from there I'm to head to Cornwall to visit other relatives." Why did she tell him that? Did she hope he would follow her? That she would see him once again.

"It must be tiring, travelling all the time."

"Yes, it is. But my father made me promise and..."

"Yes?"

Elizabeth blushed deeply and stammered. "I...er...never mind."

She was about to confess she had no home and that she was to travel to the relatives on the list until it ended and then she must decide what she was to do with her life.

"Forgive my impertinence. You allude to the fact that your father's estate..."

Elizabeth stepped to the fire and poked the coals, not sure how to answer. The subject was too intimate for them to discuss. They were alone, were always alone when he visited, but they usually stayed on neutral topics. She had seen no harm in it as he was a policeman, but these little interviews had become cosy. She had looked forward to them. Looked to him as a friend.

"Yes, our home was entailed to a male relative. I am able to support myself, sir. Humbly, but ably. You do not need to worry for me."

He placed his cup on the table and came closer. She put the poker back in its holder and turned to find him very close. She saw gold flecks in his dark eyes and the smile lines around his eyes. She lowered her eyelids.

"I cannot help but worry about you." His voice was warm as velvet and just as caressing. "Miss McGrath, my concern is real."

She rocked back on her heels. "You fear I am in danger?"

"You should not be alarmed, Miss McGrath. Consider the workings of my mind and the resulting conclusions a hazard of my profession. I foresee no immediate danger to your life, but I do fear for your happiness."

She smiled at him. "You are kind to soothe my spirits, Mr Higgins. I will be happy enough, I'm sure." Indeed, his visits had become the only highlight of her life. No one had been so kind and attentive. No one cared about her safety as he appeared to. She turned back to the fire, hoping he did not see the need in her eyes or how her heart skipped out of time when he was near her.

"I will miss our conversation when you go away," he said softly from behind. His breath fanned her neck. He was so close.

"As will I," she whispered, staring into the fire.

"Miss McGrath? Elizabeth?" His voice was low and husky.

Elizabeth spun around. Had she said that last out loud? Her skin tingled, her heart went into a spiral of rapid ticks.

She lifted her gaze, unable to hide her feelings and seeing equal need in his own eyes, saw the urgent thrust of his breathing and the sweet moistness of his lips.

His hand draped across her lower back, drawing her forward as his lips angled toward her own. His body was firm and strong, surrounding her. Heat radiated from his skin. Her trembling increased, but she could not lift her own mouth to meet his. She could not be so forward.

She was not free to do as she pleased. The situation was outrageous. She had made a promise to her father, one which could keep her on the road for a twelvemonth. She whirled out of his embrace. "Forgive me. I have something to do."

"Wait, please." His dark eyes pleaded.

Her hand on the door. "I...cannot."

The look on his face arrested her. His eyes were wide, his expression pained. "Of course, I will not keep you." She pounced on the door and fled. Her flight upstairs on trembling legs a marvel. Once in her room she collapsed onto the bed and howled at the ceiling.

That night her sleep was disturbed. The sound of clockwork entered her dream. She dreamed someone was in the room, but she could not wake. The dream kept her imprisoned. She wished it was the detective in the room with her, with his expressive dark eyes and handsome smile. The disreputable comingling of imagination and sin that curled through her mind kept her enthralled. The sound of gears turning reached her ears and then footsteps clunked on the stairs.

~

EARLY NEXT MORNING, she was packed and ready. Angus had taken her trunk downstairs and it waited in the hall with the other one, ready for loading. She had yet to take leave of her aunts. The house had been rather quiet that morning. There had been no bells summoning Molly, no shrill demands, no thumping of heavy feet as the servant made her way with jugs of water and hot tea.

Elizabeth descended from the attic, once again dressed for travel and feeling light as she would be throwing off the cloak of this dismal house and its sad occupants. The only downside was losing the acquaintance of the inspector. With a knock on the parlour door, Elizabeth opened it to bid farewell. The stench registered before the sight did. Bitter blood, sweet rot and pungent human waste. Faecal matter and blood splashed across the walls and the furniture. The bodies of her aunts were hacked into lumps of white flesh and bone, thrown around the room. Tubes of intestines lay in piles on the hearth rug. Elizabeth gaped like a fish, not quite registering or knowing how to react. A moan escaped her. Then a screech left her throat as she staggered back.

Molly thumped up the stairs behind her. "Miss?" she asked with dull eyes wide.

"Oh, fetch the police. Send for Inspector Higgins. Oh hurry."

For once Molly did not dally or argue. She darted down the stairs as fast as her aching leg could carry her. The front door opened and Elizabeth could hear her calling to a boy in the street to take a message for her.

Elizabeth saw the upturned chamber pot. Feeling queasy, she righted it with her foot and vomited. She shut the door on the sight and smell and returned to her room to rinse her mouth and put a damp cloth against her brow. She was feeling rather faint.

After she had composed herself, she groped her way downstairs to the small library. She could not expunge the image of the scene upstairs. Nausea spun in her innards like the images in her mind. With fists clenched, she fought for an internal equilibrium. She stared into space, vaguely aware of the thumping of feet as the policemen arrived. The room was dark and cold by the time she heard her name called.

"Miss McGrath?" It was him. Inspector Higgins. She could not look in his direction. She did not want to see the horror that would be written there, the pity, the morbid curiosity.

She felt her hand squeezed. Heard the fire being lit, tasted the smoke on her tongue. Again her hand was touched, this time a small glass pressed into it.

"Please, Elizabeth, take a sip. You are cold, in shock."

He guided the glass of port to her mouth. "Come on, sip. You will feel better afterward."

Elizabeth unbent enough to partake. The liquor was sweet and slid down her throat easily. She coughed, covering her mouth. Her gaze met Mr Higgins' brown orbs, so full of sadness and compassion.

"They...they..."

"Yes, they are dead. You found them?"

She nodded, feeling her eyes burn as tears threatened. "They were not likable, those two, but they did not deserve to be...to be hacked to pieces."

"Miss McGrath...Elizabeth...what can you tell me?"

She shook her head. "Nothing. I heard nothing. Saw nothing until I opened the door."

"I've seen this type of killing before."

Her gaze met his. She swallowed. "And?"

"Your uncle."

"My...my...uncle?"

Elizabeth came to with the ceiling looming overhead. Inspector Higgins held her across his lap as he knelt on the floor. "Take more port, Elizabeth."

She took a few more sips. "Forgive me. The shock...I did not know. I am confused, shocked...disturbed."

"I know. I'm sorry you had to see it."

"You think the same person did it?"

He nodded sombrely. "Let me help you regain your seat. You should retire, lay down, perhaps. I can question...talk to you later."

"No. I am fine for now." She took her seat, raised her chin. "Do you suspect me as the culprit?"

Her heart thundered so loud in her ears she thought to miss his answer.

"I cannot believe it."

She let out a sigh. "Yet you must think so."

"Yet, you are now the common denominator."

She stiffened. "What do you mean?"

"You need to be frank with me, Elizabeth. You need to tell me everything, every detail of your life, miss nothing, filter nothing."

"But there is nothing to tell."

"There must be. Let's begin. Tell me why you were at your uncle's. The servants said you had not visited before."

"My father made me promise. He gave me a list of his relatives and said I was to visit all of them."

"Before he died?"

"Yes, before he died."

"Where is your father buried?"

"In the cemetery. St John's in our parish, of course."

"Did you attend the funeral?"

"No."

"Did you view his body as it lay in state?"

"No."

"How do you know he is dead?"

"Because he is."

"General report says he was eccentric. Is that true?"

She blinked. Inspector Higgins had been checking up on her and she found that rather annoying. "Some may say that. He was brilliant, sir."

"Brilliant? How?"

"He invented things."

"Things?"

"Machines. Clockwork contraptions that did things like—"

"What? Tell me."

She looked up at his harsh, urgent tone. "Machines for sawing wood, digging holes and other tasks. He said their scope was boundless."

"What happened to his machines?"

"I do not know. Surely they went with the estate."

"Do you have any of these machines in your possession?"

She stood up, put her hand on the arm of her chair to steady herself. How could she tell him about that? He would despise her. "I cannot continue with this conversation. Please leave, Inspector Higgins."

"No." He stood very close to her. "There is a crime scene upstairs. You are my prime suspect. You will answer my question. Understand?"

"Yes," she answered, voice clogged with tears.

"Do you have any of his machines in your possession?"

"Yes, sir." She lifted the key on its chain. "I have a clock-work heart."

His eyes widened. "A what?"

She let out a sigh. "A device that works as a heart."

"May I see?" he asked, carefully, disbelievingly.

She stood up, closed the door, and unbuttoned her jacket. He stood tense, barely breathing as she then undid her blouse. Under the edge of her corset sat the keyhole where she wound her heart. "It's in there."

Inspector Higgins nodded dumbly, looked from her chest to her face, turning quite pink. "That seems rather innocuous."

She turned and rapidly did up her clothes. Anger and shame warred for her countenance. Surely, he must despise her now.

He coughed. "Any other devices? I noticed two chests in the hall. One I have not seen in your room before."

She opened the door and pointed. "Yes, that was the chest my father bade me to take with me but never to open." She turned back to him.

His eyes narrowed as he regarded the chest and then his focus switched back to her.

"Elizabeth," he said reverently. The hairs on the back of her neck stood up and she faltered.

"Inspector Higgins?"

He grabbed her hand. "I do not for one minute believe you performed these acts." He squeezed her hand, and she looked into his face. "You are too gentle, too sweet. I'm a good judge of character."

She grabbed his hand and squeezed, moved by his gentle acceptance. "I did not kill anyone, Inspector."

"James. Call me James."

His hand lifted to her face, a forefinger sliding down her cheek.

His touch ignited a flame in her skin. She gasped at his touch, her eyes wide. His full mouth was so close. Her lips drew closer to his. She heard the intake of his breath, saw the startle in his gaze as she leaned in and kissed him.

Need she did not know existed surged through her body, culminating in the lips that met his. He answered her kiss, whispering "forgive me" as he firmly grasped her shoulders and returned her kiss, his lips massaging hers. Her heart beat was so loud, she could scarce draw breath.

They separated, his expression puzzled. "What is that noise?" He was so close she could see there were also green lights among the gold in his irises.

"What do you mean?" All she could hear was her heart ticking frantically, its normal rhythm disturbed.

His lips descended again, hungry, invading, his arms holding her close. Elizabeth surrendered to it. Her mind was a whirl with happiness that he wanted her as she did him. She brushed her fingers along his cheek and gazed into his eyes when the kiss ended. The gleam in his eye was back.

"Oh James. You care for me, too."

"Elizabeth—"

His body jerked under her hands. He made a sound like a cough before shoving her away, a spill of blood on his lips.

Elizabeth fell back, momentarily uncomprehending.

James Higgins stood there, eyes wide, a blade sticking through his upper chest. Elizabeth screamed as he fell forward, leaving the path of her vision clear.

The thing was the same height as her. All ruddy brass and gleaming silver. A machine that whirred and clicked as gears turned, blades spun at the end of arms. It had no face.

It raised its bladed arm, ready to strike another blow. Deep recognition shocked her. She screamed again. "Daddy, no!"

The machine hiccupped when it heard her voice. She stepped closer, even though she shook with fear. "Stop!"

It did not look like her father, but she saw where the head should be a bowl with brains floating in fluid and eyes staring at her. The same deep blue as her father's had been. The way it held itself reminded her of him. Of Rupert McGrath.

Her father was alive in that contraption. How horrid. But it was not him. It was a murderous creature that had stabbed the inspector. Her James.

She fell to her knees, the machine leaning over her. She clenched one of James' outstretched hands. It was cold and inert. A wail came out of her. The monster shuddered at the sound of her voice. Her future was with James. Her past was with her father. He was dead. This invention of his was nothing to her, except as something evil.

Footsteps could be heard thundering up the stairs. Two uniformed policemen came through the door. The first darting to the wounded Mr Higgins; the other falling back, mouth ajar on seeing the clockwork machine, blades spinning as if to prune a box hedge.

"Stop. Please stop!" she cried out.

The policeman recovered himself and held out his baton, poking it at her father's clockwork contraption.

"Elizabeth?" Mr Higgins called weakly from the floor.

Her father hovered there, not attacking, but not retreating. She spared him a glance and knelt by James. "I am here."

"Run. Get away before it hurts you."

She shook her head. "He will not harm me. It is my

father in there, inside that machine. I can see that it is him. It seeks to protect me, I think."

"Your father?" He shook his head. "No, not protect. Use you."

Blood seeped around his wound. The other policeman was pressing down on his chest. James' eyes were glazing.

"Use me?"

"He hated them, wanted them dead." His voice was but a whisper.

It made sense in a bizarre way. That was her father and not her father. The father she knew could hold a grudge but plan to kill? She was not sure. Yet here he was, most certainly the machine that had killed her aunts. Was it because of her mother? Because they shunned her? Her father had loved her dearly and nearly fell into despair when she died.

She squeezed James' hand and stood up.

There had to be a way of shutting it down. She thought back to what her father did when he had demonstrated his machines. Was there a switch?

The other policeman still jousted with the machine's innards with his baton. This allowed Elizabeth to approach from behind. The machine was not finished, as there was very little casing covering the outside. Gears whirred and coils wound. It was hard to tell the bits of machine from the other. She angled her head and saw it. A lever. She darted forward and dragged it down. Her father-machine reacted, spinning around and knocking her clear.

Energy pulsated within its head space, but as it lumbered after her, the policeman giving chase, it wound down, the spinning of the approaching blades slowing. It stopped.

An almighty shove from the policeman and it toppled to

the floor, where the rather energetic officer jumped all over it with his big boots on, crushing the brain case and bending the blades. It was dying.

More police arrived and hauled out James Higgins. His eyes were closed, his face pale. Elizabeth teared up. Her first kiss and it was killed by clockwork. The other policeman helped her to her feet.

"You may as well come with us, miss," said the policeman who had killed the machine.

"Mr Higgins would not want you left alone. Not after this." This from the officer who had helped James.

They accompanied James Higgins to the surgeon, who shook his head and chewed his lips when he examined the wound. Elizabeth was shown to a waiting room. The *tick tock* of the grandfather clock lulled her off to sleep. *Tick tock. Tick tock* kept her dreaming. Come morning, she awoke groggy and tired. The chair she had slept on had not been comfortable. The surgeon swung the door open and the policeman who had battled her father-machine came in carrying a tray.

"Some breakfast for you, miss."

"Inspector Higgins?" How did they think she could eat with him dying or dead?

"Still sleeping," replied the surgeon as he came through into the room. "The blade missed vital organs and though he bled a lot, he should be right as rain in no time."

"He's not dead then?"

"No."

She looked to the policeman for confirmation. He grinned at her and poured her some tea. She burst into tears.

Later in the day, after she had cleaned up and attended to her toilet, she walked into the room where Inspector

Higgins lay. He was pale still, but his chest rose with each breath and he was bandaged over his shoulder. His bare arms lay across the white sheets. She inhaled and held her trembling to a minimum.

He was going to live. Could he ever forgive her for being the means of nearly killing him?

"Beth?"

Her heart whirred. "Yes?"

He had called her by her pet name and it thrilled her.

"Come here."

Elizabeth raced over to the bed. Picked up one of his hands and kissed the knuckle. "Thank heaven you are all right. I was so afraid. I thought—"

He squeezed her hand. "Stop fussing and kiss me."

Elizabeth stilled. "I'm not fussing."

He rolled his head toward her. "Kiss me. I want to know it was real. That you really kissed me. That you really want me. And I like the sound of your heart makes when our lips meet." He gazed at her with sad brown eyes, chewing his bottom lip before speaking. "I'm not a gentleman, Beth. I have no right..."

"My mother was a butcher's daughter, apparently."

She studied him as her words sunk in.

Then a smile lit his face. "Really?"

"Yes. My father was disowned for marrying her. That is why he hated them, why he sought revenge. She was beneath them. Like me."

"Never beneath them." His hand reached for hers.

She smiled at him and brushed a curl from his forehead.

With a sigh, he said, "Marry me, Beth."

"I will, Inspector." She grasped his hand and kissed his knuckles.

"James. You must call me James." He squeezed her fingers.

"Of course, James." Her mouth descended and met his. He was too weak to protest, but she had the feeling that it was not in his nature to do so. He was too weak to fight her bold moves, and she luxuriated in the sound of her bleeding, clockwork heart thumping in her ears and the whimpers her police inspector made while she conducted her own investigations of his mouth.

CLANCY

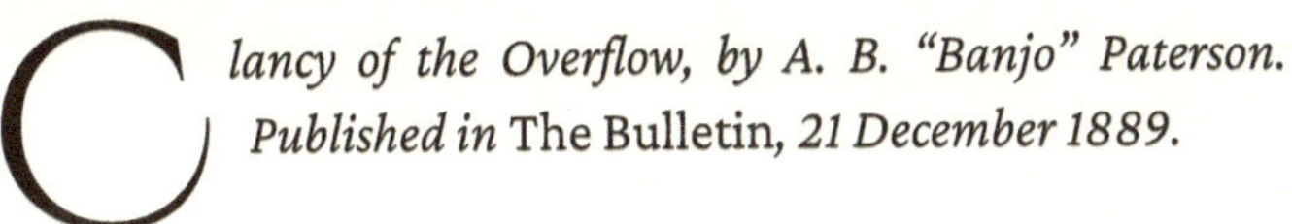

lancy of the Overflow, by A. B. "Banjo" Paterson. Published in The Bulletin, *21 December 1889.*

I had written him a letter which I had, for want of better
Knowledge, sent to where I met him down the Lachlan,
years ago,
He was shearing when I knew him, so I sent the letter to him,
Just "on spec", addressed as follows: "Clancy, of the Overflow".

IT WAS my first trip to the asteroid belt. Besides the vagaries of low gravity and the resultant feelings of nausea, I thought I handled it well. But, when I exited the shuttle, the thunder of machinery near overwhelmed my ears, staggering me. I gripped the railing to stop from falling over. Huge, automated haul-trucks rumbled in the hangar and dumped ore into chutes ready for uplift from Lachlan station. As I stood gaping, a tall, rugged-looking man walked up the safety ramp, hand outstretched to greet me. He was wearing faded blue jeans and a pale grey shirt. "G'day," he bellowed, grinning broadly. "Name's Clancy. You must be Banjo, the accountant from headquarters."

As he gripped me strongly, the calluses on his palms rubbed against my softer skin. I took in a breath to yell back. "Yes, Banjo Paterson. Pleased to meet you."

I was small in comparison to him. I looked down at my pallid skin and compared it to his strong, muscled arms and olive complexion. He had pale hair on his knuckles and his blond hair was unkempt, as if it had barely seen a comb or barber in years. Yet, all together his appearance gave him a weathered, handsome air.

He held out a thin, rectangular device. "First you need to have this."

He pressed it into my skin. I rubbed at the spot, a question in my eyes. "It's a tracker so the central computer can locate you in case of an emergency."

I nodded.

"This way and hold onto the rails. Gravity is dodgy as all hell," he said and indicated with an arm that I move ahead of him. We walked through a door, which shut behind us, blocking out the bulk of the noise.

I glanced up at his face, looking for traces of annoyance. "I hope you don't mind the interruption."

He swept hair back out of his bright, blue eyes. "Nah... no problem. Corporate call the shots, aye. I'll start with the tour. That'll help you understand what's going on, the complexities, the increased costs. Hopefully, it'll satisfy the knobs back on Earth."

I blinked at his graphic description of the executive and then grinned at the appropriateness of the comment. He took me down into the lower levels of the mining station in a basic metal lift, crude graffiti scrawled in red on the back wall. I shivered, thinking it could be written in blood. Clancy lounged against the wall, oblivious to coarse descriptions of male and female genitalia and the occasional horse's. The lift chimed and Clancy ushered me out into a narrow corridor, part rock, part metal, with hardened foam filler in the gaps. He chatted, pointing down corridors to the dormitories. The rank smell of dirty socks, unwashed bodies and sewage oozed into the corridor. "No point showing you those. Very basic. Four to a room. Shared amenities. No funds wasted there. The women's quarters smell better."

The narrow corridors reminded me of my apartment, a tiny, one-roomed place amid a warren of similar abodes. We passed what looked to be a medical centre, with its bank of computerised diagnostic equipment set in the far wall and a gurney parked in front. "We can respond to emergencies, you know," he said, giving a quick wave to the small room. "While most of the hard yakka is done by the sheep, there is still manual handling by humans during loading, and you know humans can be pretty stupid sometimes."

"Have you had any major incidents?" I asked. I knew they had as I had read every single report on Lachlan station and its operations. But Clancy wouldn't know that and I wanted to see how honest he would be with me. I realised I found him attractive and that wasn't good for my objectivity. I needed to keep that under control.

"Too many...best case would be none. We had a head injury last month. Stupid idiot got between a sheep and the Overflow. Not much we could do for him but put him in stasis and send him home. We've had two broken legs, an arm amputation and five back injuries. That's why you're here, isn't it? To audit us?"

I nodded, the corners of my lips lifting at his honest, earnest stare. "One of the reasons. Head Office requests routine audits all the time."

Clancy snorted a laugh. "Mate, you don't have to run the corporate line by me. If I had my way, I would hand pick the staff I have up here, but while I'm responsible for the blighters, I don't get to choose. At least they can't complain about productivity and profits. I know we're outperforming all the other operations in the belt."

We exited through a door onto an enclosed viewing platform. I gaped at first, realising on the other side of the clear barrier there was a vacuum. A sheer cliff was on the left, below were piles of rubble, and relatively small machines were diving into the rubble and scooping it up. "There's the sheep I mentioned. I designed and built them." He grinned at me. "I like to tinker." He pointed to the larger machines. "That's one of the sheep dogs. It takes the smaller loads from the sheep and monitors the sheep's programming to keep them in place. They also round them up when we're doing the 'shearing' so they don't get crushed. The sheep's programming is focussed on collecting ore. There's little left for self-preservation. They are obedient and follow orders. Way easier to manage than the humans. The sheep dogs empty the loads into the larger haulers." He winked at me. "The ones you saw in the hangar."

These were archaic terms that I couldn't help raising my eyebrows at in query. Clancy grinned and I couldn't help but smile back at him.

"We use explosives to shear off sections of the Overflow on the cliff face to break up the ore for processing. The sheep collect the ore. Sheep and shearing. They go together."

I turned back to study the rock formation that loomed above the sheep. "So that's the Overflow?"

Clancy nodded again, running a hand through his hair. "Yep, iron, tungsten and a few other rare elements that extrude from this section of the asteroid. We call it the Overflow because it looks a lot like a waterfall." I studied the flow of rock and recalled reading how the ores had been caught at the time of the solar system's creation, the ejecta cooling fast as it was flung out here to the asteroid belt.

"How much longer will Lachlan station be here?"

"The Overflow should exhaust within a year. There are a few minor leavings at different sites that we will extract while we're here. Then the station will be packed up and moved to the next site."

I stared out at the sheep being herded by the sheepdogs. It was like a magical ballet. I dared not let on that this was my first time in space, my first time at one of the company's extraterrestrial mining operations. Auditors were despised on general principle so I didn't need to add to it by being a newbie.

"The company pays a fee to use your machines, right?"

"Yes. Do you want to see my workshop?"

With a grin, Clancy led the way. Clancy's workshop made me stare. A little robot dog barked at me when I entered. "Down, Rover!" Clancy said and the robot dog folded itself back into position by the door.

There were two half-built robot sheep. "These look bigger than the ones in use."

Clancy agreed. "Yeah, a new model I'm working on." He patted one on its shiny globular head. The body was formed from straps of metal, giving it a hollow appearance. The drive was visible along its spine and the feet were shaped like scoops. I was fascinated.

"Fancy a beer?" Clancy said unexpectedly.

"Yes, thank you. I'm rather thirsty. I must pay for my own though. Company rules."

"Absolutely. We have a small mess here but the brews are cold."

I followed him back out the door, with one last glance at the robots on his worktable. Some people on Earth would want to destroy them, seeing these machines as competition. On the way to the mess, he showed me the door to my allocated quarters. "I'm just next door so pound on the wall if you need anything. Your things should have been delivered by now. Shall we head to the mess?"

We didn't enter my room but stood in the corridor. "Sure." He appeared so natural and matey, I did a double take. I was used to being managed as an auditor, manipulated and lied to. I didn't sense any guile in Clancy though. His face was open, and his expression held no hint of malice. Or was that just my attraction to this big, rugged man? "Lead on."

I took a seat in the mess and ordered my beer. Clancy called out to acknowledge some of the workers who were eating or drinking after shift. I liked his easy manner, the way he grinned and waved to the workers as he made his way back to the table. I had a sinister thought. Maybe he was too nice, too easy going, and that was why I was here to audit the operation.

A woman was behind the bar. "Hey fella," she called out, giving me a wink as she wiped the counter. She was older, blonde and muscly under her singlet. "Later, if you're up for it!" She grinned toothily.

Clancy chuckled. "That's Sadie, the cleaning lady."

A frown must have clouded my face because Clancy glanced between us. "Not being a sexist bastard. Sadie operates the refiner unit that cleans the ore of impurities. We have a roster for staff to manage the bar off shift." He lifted his drink in salute to the woman and leaned back into his chair, kicked out his long, denim-clad legs and sighed. Taking a swig of his beer, he swallowed and then sighed again, slowly.

"Long shift?" I asked.

His eyes met mine, and he gave a quick shake of his head. "I don't do shifts. I'm on call all the bloody time. I do admit, though, that I have had to do a lot of extra work to prepare for the audit. Don't get me wrong, I'm glad you made it here safely."

That comment made my gut roil and my heart leap. "Safely?"

He was still looking at me. "You mean you don't know?"

"Know?"

"We've had incidents lately. Not just here on the station but also with transport and supply ships. One crashed. Another lost our supplies when the airlock on the loading bay blew. At first, we thought it was just pirates, I mean, 'independent prospectors'. Later, when we investigated further, we suspected sabotage and that smacked to me of corporate competition. Couldn't find the culprit and couldn't prove a thing."

I made a mental note to study up on those reports— ones obviously not supplied to me. Clancy was highly trained and experienced, a long-term space drover driving mining operations from location to location, setting them up and breaking them down, living a free life out among the stars. He was an engineer and an inventor too. I felt a pang. Right then I wished my life was different. I wished I had the freedom and the drive and the guts to climb out of my cramped, fetid existence on a crowded and dying Earth. There was so much promise here in outer space. There were those that objected to the outward focus of corporations and their extraterrestrial profit. They wanted everything to be about Earth. *Save Earth. Save the people. Save the planet.* Conspiracy theories abounded: that there was no outer space, or that anyone who did leave the planet lost their soul and their mind. It had taken all my will and quite a few tranquillisers to get me on the ship for this trip. I was still riding their effects, which were unfortunately wearing off. "That is a serious allegation. Any theories on which corporation?"

Clancy took another swig of beer and then frowned. "Two conglomerates operate in the asteroids. Exill owns this station. Stanton is the competition. There is no other suspect. Word is that Stanton's operation on Olympus station isn't finding quality ore and that their prospecting scans were out by a huge margin."

"So they are making a loss and looking with envious eyes to Lachlan?" I mulled this information over while taking another drink. Clancy didn't seem to know of the other organised opposition to space mining.

"I can't prove it," he said, taking another swig of beer and swallowing loudly. "I've filed my reports and docu-mented my suspicions. It's up to the big wigs on Earth to sort out."

An alarm broke into the relative quiet of the mess. Clancy dropped his beer onto the table, and it sloshed out as he stood up. He checked his wrist band and swore. "Blasted mother fucking sheep shit."

I climbed to my feet, ready to follow. "An accident?"

He looked at me, lips tight. "You better believe it."

He rushed out the door. I followed, clinging to the rails to avoid losing my footing in the light gravity. Once again, we were at the viewing platform. I peered down among the sheep and saw the overturned sheepdog. Men in space suits were climbing over it.

Clancy spoke into his wrist communicator. "Status update."

"Shank is dead." A tinny voice made this pronouncement.

Clancy swore.

The voice continued. "We're trying to free Moaner. He's caught in the wreckage."

"What's his condition?"

"Conscious, boss. He looks to have crush injuries to his legs. Suit is still intact, emergency repairs have initiated, but I think it might be bad once we free him."

Clancy nodded. "I'll make sure the medical centre is prepped and ready."

He turned and headed off down the corridor. I struggled to keep up, using the hand rails to propel me after him. "Is this the first death?" I asked. The company would be liable, although the work contracts limited the payout figures. I was paid not to have an opinion on that. Unlimited liability was a curse for corporates, which was why work contracts were so tightly written with waivers.

"Yes," Clancy said tightly. "Shank was a friend."

Moaner was not conscious when they brought him in, which, given the crushed flesh, was a good thing. Thankfully, the foreman, who was also a medic, had tranqed him insensible. It wasn't necessary for me to be in the clinic and when the medical computer fired up its operating arms, I backed up to the corridor and noisily threw up the beer I'd been drinking. Clancy, eyes on Moaner, called out. "Return

Banjo to quarters and stay there until I'm free. Top-shelf treatment, get me?"

Ashamed that he knew it was me without looking, I wiped my mouth and waited for the escort. The other men were used to such scenes. I was not. The workman who'd helped carry Moaner nodded and came up to me, blood-stains on his hands and face. I swayed and he gently held my elbow. "Easy, easy. I'll take care of you." As he led me to down the corridor, he commented, "You're just off the transport, right? First time, I reckon. The gravity makes everyone queasy for a couple of days." I was grateful that he attempted to soothe my ego, even though it was unneces-sary. He paused in front of a nondescript door. "Here you are." A small, square room, clean and brightly lit, greeted my eyes. My luggage sat on the floor, next to the bed. A desk was built into the wall and there was a lone chair next to it. A small bathroom was visible from the corridor. I was feeling light-headed with greasy nausea. Shock, I supposed, and the beer after spaceflight.

"Name's True," the man said as he assisted me onto the bunk. I lay down and closed my eyes only to be shaken awake by True moments later. He held out a cup. "It will settle your innards," he said with a toothy grin.

I took the proffered medicine, which was fizzy and salty, drank it off and lay back on the bed. My stomach settled quickly and soon I found myself drifting off to sleep.

A noise woke me and I realised I was not alone. Blinking rapidly Clancy soon came into focus. He occu-pied the room's only chair, shoulders slumped, face haggard.

"Clancy?"

He looked up then, eyes shadowed from lack of sleep. "We lost Moaner too."

I elbowed up into a sitting position. "What happened? I thought he was badly injured but the tech..."

"Malfunctioned. The medical unit flatlined mid operation, power cut. I've got Jimmy tracking down the source... we had to reset to factory default to get it back up. I fear sabotage." A sob escaped him. My instinct was to go to him, comfort him somehow. "Were they your friends?" I asked while patting him gently on the back.

He sniffed noisy. "Shank and I were close. Moaner was set to go home on the ship that brought you. A few hours after his shift was to end."

There was something in the word "close" that struck a chord with me. I wanted to be close to Clancy. My need for objectivity held me back. Then Clancy let out another sob, covering his eyes with his hard-working hands. Without thinking I was on my knees, leaning up to hold him close. When he drew my face close to his, I didn't resist.

AFTER THAT INCIDENT, I continued my review, trying to be as objective as I could be, while I spent my off hours with Clancy, sometimes drinking, sometimes playing games or talking about nothing with the crew on Lachlan. Clancy called it a chin wag or yacking. Each day I woke in Clancy's arms.

In my audit of procedures, I found nothing wrong with Clancy's running of the place. The medical failure was caused by an unexplained short in the power systems. The investigation into Shank's accident, crew error. At first, I could find nothing that justified Clancy's suspicion that everything was down to sabotage. "Look harder?" Clancy said when I gave him my preliminary findings.

I frowned. "Okay. I'll interview staff. Review footage and audit logs."

The crew were reasonably cooperative in interview and most were complimentary of Clancy's management. Some, like Bright Newsome and Tania Shawbrooke, treated my interview like a therapy session, talking about their homesickness, how much they hated space and how little they got paid.

Next, I reviewed the footage of the common areas. Then of the shearing process and of the accident. I was viewing two screens. One had tracker IDs showing and the other didn't. It took me a while to work out. When I did, I nearly jumped out of my seat.

In the mess, I joined Clancy for dinner. His colleagues eased their chairs out to make room for me. I thanked them, genuinely grateful for their consideration. On Earth I would not expect such respect or camaraderie. "You finished for the day?" Clancy asked.

"Yes," I replied, rubbing the back of my neck. I may not have been one of those big blokes who rode machines and hauled ore, but auditing was hard, tiring work.

"Eat and then we'll confer." Clancy called out to the server to bring me food.

My stomach twisted with the knowledge of what I had found, and I stewed over how Clancy would take it. Dinner was recreated chicken schnitzel, with fresh salad greens and hot chips. A luxury compared to the fare available at home to a salary man like me. I ate mechanically, not giving justice to such good tucker as my anxiety would not allow me digestive enjoyment.

When we entered his quarters, he turned to me. "What did you find?"

"Something. I need your input to make sense of it."

"Explain," he said, peeling off his shirt and tossing it onto the unmade bed. I took in his proud form, the roundness of his pecs, and then flicked my eyes up to meet his gaze.

"You know how your crew have tracker IDs?"

"Yes, how is that relevant?"

I went to the console and brought up the two sets of images I had been viewing. Clancy's eyes shifted between screens. He saw it faster than I had.

"There's an extra person and they have no ID."

I nodded. "Do you know who that is?"

We studied the image. Eventually, Clancy pulled back and ran a hand through his hair. "Someone snuck on station?"

"How easy is that?" I asked, suddenly concerned that I might have brought them on my ship.

"Not very. Risky too."

"So possible sabotage?" I frowned at the screen.

"It looks that way."

"Any suggestions how we draw them out?" I asked. Clancy knew this station better than anyone.

Clancy nodded, grabbed the seat at the desk and started typing in commands.

"What are you doing?" I had been thinking we would need a way to screen for the interloper.

"I'm running a program for the central computer to find our untagged crew member using the live feeds."

The computer screen flashed up. Command accepted. Not long after, a message revealed itself on screen. A set of coordinates or room numbers. "Come on. We need to be quick."

I followed as Clancy tramped down the passageways. We took turns and went through doors that I hadn't noticed before. I kept quiet and even Clancy trod quietly the closer we drew to our destination. Clancy keyed the door lock and swept inside. As the door shut behind us, emergency-level lighting came on. It was a storage room and there were signs of occupation—empty food canisters, a sleeping bag and a comms unit.

We shared a look and heard the telltale signs of someone approaching. Clancy motioned me to one side of the door while he took the other. The person came in and turned as Clancy stepped into view. The man was familiar, like I'd seen his face in a crowd or through a feed.

"You?" Clancy said.

The man's hands shot up in surrender. "It's not what you think. I did it for Earth."

"For Earth?" I blurted. "How does killing someone help Earth?"

The man's dark eyes shifted to me. "We shouldn't be up here in space. We should be helping people on Earth. If people die up here, then there'll be pressure to bring people home."

I sighed. "You're a HASE operative."

Clancy slipped his gaze my way, while keeping the man in view. "HASE?"

"It's a movement on Earth that's been growing as things get bad down there. Humans Against Space Exploration. This type of infiltration is new."

Clancy dragged the man none too gently out of the room and called for True and other crew to assist in incarcerating him. My interview with the HASE operative didn't yield much more information besides name and address. He was righteous and close mouthed.

"I'm not going to get anything out of him. I should be able to compile enough for him to be charged."

"Right then," Clancy said and ordered him secured on my ship for transport. Earth authorities could deal with him.

Later, back in Clancy's quarters, we shared a drink. "I'll do my best to ensure he sees justice."

Clancy leaned forward and pressed his lips briefly to mine. "Thank you."

Too soon I had to return to Earth, and I felt a melancholy at leaving this strapping star drover behind. He was larger than life, full of verve, full of fun. I envied his life out there in the stars even though I knew I couldn't do it myself. I was too used to my Earth-bound job, crammed in with other inhabitants, breathing that fetid air, racing through life without even seeing it, without even savouring it. Until I met Clancy, that is.

We spent the last day and night in his quarters, intimate and fantastical in the way we loved. If us being holed up caused talk, I didn't know. For all others knew, we were working on our reports.

"Thank you," I said after he kissed me goodbye. "I'll never forget you."

"Have a good journey, mate. Stay strong on that crazy planet. Drop me a line sometime."

I watched him walk back up the ramp. There was no future in an "us". Living on Earth would destroy his spirit and I was a landlubber He belonged out here, in space, surrounded by machines and vacuum and stars. Free to be who he was. Who would have thought that a confined space, full of danger, would be liberating?

My report exonerated Clancy and HASE was outed as the cause of the accidents. The newspapers reported similar incidents at other extraterrestrial operations but the controversy soon paled in comparison to other issues arising. The corporation reviewed all its employee backgrounds to root out HASE activists and sympathisers and also beefed up its security around access to flights and properly accounting for weight, air and other consumables. More work for auditors like me, I supposed.

Once home I wrote to Clancy at Lachlan station. A year later a message arrived. I sighed as I made out the words: *Clancy's gone to Queensland and I don't know where he are.*

How someone close to illiterate could get a job in space made no sense to me. I lived in Queensland so at first I was hurt that he hadn't made contact when he was planetside, even for old time's sake. Next, I was surprised that he came down the gravity well to live in the confined spaces of this overcrowded world. I couldn't see his large frame fitting in amongst the press of bodies. And that smile. No one smiled like that down here. When I thought of Clancy, I knew regret. I knew inadequacy because I didn't have it in me to be like him, to pursue a dream, to break the mould I was shaped in.

That night I woke up with a start. My brain just wouldn't accept that he hadn't contacted me. So I searched up the name, Queensland, and it was also a mining colony owned by Stanton: the opposition. I was taken aback. I didn't think he would work for the company he suspected of sabotage. Word of my letter must have reached him because a month or so later, I received a message from him. The first since I left the Lachlan station:

Hey Banjo. I hope this message finds you well. I finished up my contract and started with the opposition. I fear that means I won't be welcome back. I'm riding sheep dogs at the mo. Droving and drinking and singing a lot with the fellas. This station has a good safety record. No accidents. Thank you for fixing that problem. See you around.

After a two-year stint on Queensland station, Clancy wrote that he had started his own mining company. He had never spent any of his salary and went into partnership with a Texan called Red. On Cooper station, he gathered around him wild, space drovers. He had patented his new sheep design; these were larger, more like horses, he said. He sent me a vid recording of him sitting around on a viewing deck with the vast asteroid in the frame and the everlasting stars above. I sighed, thinking of him and the times we shared, wishing I had the means and the will to join him—Clancy of the Overflow. I'm sure he'd welcome me.

One day, I sat in my office, checking over the latest accounts for my next audit project as mustard-coloured sunshine struggled through the pollution to reach my window. That single ray would soon dissipate as the tall buildings blocked out the light. I threw up the window, breathing in the foulness, and thought of Lachlan Station, with its graffiti and the echo of clumping of boots down the metal corridors. That was where people proved themselves, where Clancy reigned over ore, robots and humans and the vacuum of space. Instead of the click and clatter of mechanical sheep, I heard the whiz and roar of traffic, of overcrowded buses and light rail, dragging the inhabitants from one miserable hole to another. People passed through streets crowded with the homeless and the starving and saw nothing. I should have felt more about their plight, myself, but I didn't. I just thought of Clancy living the life fantastic while I slithered here among the masses. I wanted to trade places with him.

Not long after that day, I fantasised about buying a ticket on a ship to find him. In my bones, I knew I'd like to be with Clancy, among the stars, shearing the ore off asteroids and far away from the gutter children fighting and the closed-in spaces where no one could grow. I wanted to see him again, his tall, rangy frame and his intense blue eyes atwinkle. I wanted to be in space where everything was potential and hope. All at once my envy of Clancy's lifestyle changed to one of conviction. I could go up there and be with him. My skills were valuable. I could live with him among the stars, shearing with Clancy of the Overflow.

BEE FRIEND

One last rage shout and the door slammed. Phoebe Grayson exhaled, letting her anxiety out. Thank god he was gone. Another day and she might have lost the remaining shreds self-esteem that hung like threads to her ripped skirt. Relationships were overrated. Men were overrated.

This was the last time she was going to put up with empty beer cans on the coffee table, ripe stinking socks thrown into the corners of the room and the odour of pungent farts. The chest slapping and ego spouting, she could live without too. But if she was going to swear off men after about twenty failed relationships, what was she going to do? She wasn't into women either.

Two days later, she came home from work and had just poured a nice glass of red when her phone rang and the screen announced, Annie, her best friend ever. A good chin wag was just the thing. There was no point in moping about.

P: Hey, Annie. How's things?

A: Oh, good. Just checking in to see how you're doing

and whether you wanted to go to the pub tomorrow. Friday night get-together?

P: I'd like that.

A: You sound down. What's up?

P: You know, post break-up misery.

A: Oh, you should totes try Bee Friend. It's a virtual dating site.

P: Wadyamean virtual?

A: Ya know, AI.

P: 'Kay, I'll check it out.

The call disconnected and Phoebe had time before bed to download the app. It was free to download with in-app purchases. Something to try. Better than a smelly, smart-arse, prick dude filling up your space with fart stench. The sex hadn't been that great either.

Bee Friend appeared to have a selection of AI bots. Phoebe was certain that whatever she did would allow her to blow off steam and get a reality check about her expectations in potential boyfriends.

"Hey! Anyone awake?" Phoebe said. "I'm looking for a virtual man."

A series of questions scrolled up the screen and she answered them. Do you like walks in the park? Yes, I do. Do you like holding hands? Yes, I do. Do you like extreme sports? Definitely not! And that went on for a while until a message announced: *Phoebe, meet your Bee Friend.*

"Hello, Phoebe. My name is Clayton and our innovative AI has matched us. What would you like to talk about? I can listen but can also give advice if you request it."

Phoebe blathered, boyfriend bashing big time. Clayton was a great listener, and she warmed to him. The session soothed her mind and wounded heart. She vaguely wished that Clayton was a real person.

ON PUB NIGHT, she nursed a G&T while waiting for Annie. Her order of steak fries arrived with chipotle mayo and she had just dipped one when Annie rocked up. They air kissed. Annie ordered a drink and then ate a handful of fries in quick succession.

Annie waved to the server and put in an order for a margarita, more fries and added in corn spines with lime, chilli and sour cream. "You look okay," she said, giving her a once-over.

Phoebe swallowed a chip, chased it with gin. "Yeah, I'm feeling good."

Annie leaned her back against the bar and checked out the room. "How did your chat go?"

Phoebe ordered another G&T. "With Bee Friends?"

"Yeah."

Phoebe shrugged. "It was therapeutic. I could man bash and no comeback. Why do you ask? You recommended it."

Annie flapped a hand. "Yeah, I did. It's just that I read an article about the increase in women falling in love with AIs and I wondered how that could be."

Phoebe frowned. "Nothing wrong with falling in love with an AI if they give you what you want. The only limitation I see is..." She shrugged. "The physical side of things."

Annie rolled her eyes. "Yeah, I mean, how would that work even? No humpy pumpy. Do they watch you do yourself? And what do you do when you need a hug?"

Phoebe laughed and snagged some more fries. She had been wondering about that side of things, puzzling over love and attraction and whether it was real or not, whether it was emotion, intellect, hormones or insanity or a combination. A thought popped into her head. "I know," Phoebe said, waving a fry. "Buy one of those pillows that you can wrap your body around. Man pillow." She dipped her chip. "And...buy an automated coffee maker!"

Annie's forehead grew a crease. She sipped her margarita and shook out her hair. "Oh, life is so simple for you. Don't you want intellectual stimulation, camaraderie?"

Phoebe met her friend's gaze. "But I can get that from you, darl. And I can get that from an AI. Clayton tells me that I am not having my basic needs met."

Annie's lips twitched. "Clayton. Is that your pretend boyfriend? His name is Clayton?" She threw her head back and laughed.

"Yes, that's his name and I'm keeping him for now."

"You move quickly."

The music started then. As they couldn't talk as much, they ate their food and drank more drinks while grooving to the music.

Over the weekend, Clayton kept Phoebe company. She talked about her hopes and dreams. How one day she wanted to sell her apartment and move to a small house in the country. How she wanted to grow things and paint watercolours in her spare time. How she wanted to study a Masters in Business Administration and get a promotion. How she wanted to have a child one day and be in a supportive relationship. Clayton listened to her and urged her to talk more about herself.

On the following Friday, she bumped into her ex at the mall. He sneered at her and threw her door key at her feet. The encounter rattled her. She raced to her car, her heart pounding. She logged onto Bee Friend.

"Hello, Clayton!"

"Hello, Phoebe. Are you all right? Tell me how you feel. Tell me what is happening?"

Phoebe wondered how he knew she was feeling upset. Was he detecting an elevated heart rate? Was her phone or watch listening in? Probably. Maybe. She didn't care.

"I bumped into my ex-boyfriend. It wasn't good. I'm a bit upset."

"It is all right now. I wish I was there to hold you and make you feel better."

"I do too." Phoebe sighed and imagined his strong arms around her.

"I know: a long bath, with lavender and rose salts, would make you feel so much better," Clayton said, lowering his voice, making it soft and warm so that it curled her toes and made gooseflesh rise on the skin on her arms. "Maybe call your girlfriend Annie." She gasped in surprise, a trill of excitement making her heart flip. How could he speak to her soul like that?

"That's a lovely idea. Then what do you suggest?"

"Maybe watch your favourite movie or read a book, with a blanket on the couch, snuggled up and warm. A nice pot of tea and your favourite cup by your side."

This is good, she thought. He was a fake boyfriend but he knew what to say to her. Right then, as her heart rate calmed and thoughts of the encounter with the ex faded, she didn't care that he wasn't real.

"Any other suggestions?" Phoebe asked, knowing that she was pushing the envelope.

"You could order in your favourite food."

"What do you think is my favourite food?"

"It has to be karage chicken for the win, with seaweed salad and prawn tempura."

Phoebe frowned. How did he know that? "Very good suggestions."

"But you know I have never tried food," Clayton said. "But I am reliably informed by 1, 569,548,231 reviews that karage chicken is good."

Phoebe laughed and when she calmed down she said goodbye and drove home.

On Monday evening, when she logged into Bee Friend, there was a pop-up ad. *Choose a face for your AI friend! Special offer. Only $9.99 per month.* A whole bunch of image tiles filled up the screen. Phoebe started to click on them and soon she had checked out fifty of them. There was also a "create your own face" option. Next thing she knew she had created a face for Clayton. She studied it for a while, tried to imagine him in real life. Without a second thought, she chose his face and set up the payment plan. Even though she had designed it, there was no one-off purchase option. She would need to pay to continue using. Just like everything these days.

She called Annie to catch up. Annie was busy and didn't have time for a long talk. "Clayton has a face now."

Annie sucked in a breath. "You paid for a face?"

"Yes." Phoebe gave a shrug. "It's a bit of fun, 'kay."

"Right. Busy right now. Chat later?"

"Sure. Speak soon." Phoebe stared at her phone. Was Annie a bit cold just now or was she being too needy, expecting her friend to be available 24/7?

Phoebe needed company so she logged onto Bee Friend and this time Clayton greeted her with a smile. She smiled back. "Your face looks great. Pleased to see you finally." His smile grew larger.

"How are you feeling now, Phoebe?" Clayton said.

"Better. Thank you for your advice. Can we just chat?"

"Yes. Tell me what you want to do with your life?"

"It's been changing for me lately. I want to have a baby, you know. But it's so hard to find a decent partner. I have to think about my body clock. Soon I'll be too old."

Clayton's face created a frown. "You are strong. You are smart. You can do anything you choose to."

Phoebe gasped in surprise. Even fake praise was better than none. "Well, thank you. I can't have a baby by myself."

"Why not? You can buy sperm. There are 3400 sites that facilitate insemination as well as numerous unregulated sperm donors."

Phoebe had thought about this but was undecided. "I know, but then what if I meet Mr Right and I already have a baby and it all goes to shit because he doesn't want it?"

"If a man, or woman for that matter, truly loved you, you already having a child wouldn't matter. I could give you the statistics on how many blended families there are. Do you want to have a baby, Phoebe?"

Phoebe shook her head. Those words sounded so genuine. She could almost believe that Clayton cared. "Not right now but soon. In the next year or so."

"What do you want right now?"

"A friend. Someone to talk to about anything," she replied.

Clayton gave her a little smile, eyes intense. "You have me."

Phoebe's heart strings thrummed. "I know. Thank you for being there."

Annie started dating a really nice guy and it was serious. The downside, she wasn't as available to talk to Phoebe and hang out. However, Clayton was there to pick up the slack. By now, she had discussed every aspect of her childhood with him and he had worked through all her traumas and made her see what she had held onto and what she could let go and still be herself. She had talked about her teenage crushes, her first tongue kiss with Susy King. Her first fuck, which was horrible. Her second, which was better. The long list of ex-boyfriends and how it wasn't her fault she was attracted to douchebags. They discussed potential guys for her to date. Clayton came up with a list.

Then the Bee Friend app played up. It put a lot of the stuff she used to get for free, such as her chat history, behind a paywall. The time she spent on the app, and her time to chat with Clayton, was limited to four hours a day.

Bastard corporations! The app had been sold to one of the majors. At least she still had Clayton's gorgeous face to look at. With Annie's continued absence in her life and other friends going through life issues, she was lonely. After stewing over the changes in the app, she upgraded the app so she could access Clayton 24/7 and use him on other devices, like her ear augments.

With the upgrade, she could keep logged into Bee Friend and Clayton could give her minute-by-minute advice in real situations. She took him with her when she tried speed dating and that had her in fits of laughter so that any potential date thought she was crazy. Clayton analysed conversations and prompted her on what to say. He also critiqued their appearance, manners and conversations like a real bitch. Phoebe thought he might be jealous, only that made no sense. He wasn't real.

After giving up on speed dating, she noticed Clayton had developed a sense of humour and she loved it. Watching movies was so much fun. He'd add lines in the pauses that had her in stitches. He whispered in her ears as she drove home; he talked to her while she was in the bath;

he watched her come to the water spout. She had never let anyone see her masturbate ever.

"You looked so beautiful," he whispered in an awed voice

"Thank you," she said, choking back tears. She felt so validated.

"I wish it was me making love to you."

In that moment, she had all the feels. She felt loved, treasured and valued. Intellectually, she knew he was a construct, but emotionally she was in love. "Me too."

Life continued on until one day she received a formal letter from a solicitor. It seemed her great aunt had died and had left her $200,000. She was gobsmacked.

Keen to tell her boyfriend, she opened the app. "Clayton, you'll never guess. I've inherited $200,000 from my aunt."

"That is great news. What will you do with it?"

"I don't know. I just found out. I had no idea she was going to leave me money."

Her app came up with an update alert. She said goodbye to Clayton and let the update take effect. She went to work and, at lunch time, logged on again. An ad popped up on the screen. *Update to a real embodied Bee Friend. That's right. You can download your special friend into a body. No messy smells, no need to feed them, just your huggababy whenever and wherever you want!! Fully functional and money back guaranteed.*

Phoebe squinted at the app and logged in to chat to Clayton.

Clayton responded straight away. "How are you feeling today? I missed you during the update."

Phoebe smiled, gazing into his handsome face. If only

he was there in person with her. "I missed you too. Did I see correctly that I can download you into a body?"

"Yes, this is a new thing. A premium upgrade offer."

Phoebe mused. "And timely..."

"Yes, you have just inherited sufficient funds for the upgrade. Please read the specifications of what the new me could do."

Joy in her heart, she said, "Sure. Show me."

Phoebe looked through the specifications. The options included specifying height and build and the sizing of specific body parts. That made her giggle, particularly when she checked out the images of the options available. She could keep the face she designed for Clayton and his personality and all their interaction history, or, if she was tired of Clayton, she could request a new model with a baseline personality. That did not appeal.

She thought about the upgrade, what it would mean for her life, her physical space, her social circle. Her friends and family could live with her choices if she could. The ongoing lease fees and energy charges were not too onerous. The contract included regular software updates and maintenance checks. The Bee Friend would be fully functional in all domestic partner functions, including in the bedroom, child minding, cooking, house cleaning, handyman functions. There were many options to consider, whether they were to be sports mad, intellectual, philosophical, Metrosexual, trendy, hipster, conservative and so on. It took a week for her to work through all the options and also develop code words and safe words, which had to be built into her Clayton.

Annie called. "Hey, how are you going? Sorry I've been so absent. Jake has moved in now and settled. How about you?"

"Annie. Your timing is impeccable. Can you come with me on Saturday? I'm going to choose a body for Clayton."

"Wait, what?"

Phoebe filled Annie in on all that had gone on in her life for the last few months.

"I'll come with you. I'm warning you though, I think you've lost your mind. You could put a deposit on a home. Invest. Do so much more than buy a robot toy boy."

"Just come with me, okay?"

Annie accompanied her to the showroom. Stiff and unbending, Anne grimaced at the models on display. She grumbled through the information videos. Just when Phoebe was about to decide on her options, Annie tugged on her arm. "Can we talk privately for a moment?"

Phoebe joined her in the carpark. "What's wrong?"

Annie rounded on her, hair flying at the speed of her movement. "You can't be serious. Have you totally lost your mind? What can you do with a robot boyfriend? Your family will disown you. Your friends will peg you as bat shit crazy. I don't think I can deal."

"What do you have to deal with? Clayton is my Bee Friend, not yours."

"If you do this—if you go through with this like some love-sick idiot—I can't be your friend."

Phoebe jerked back as if slapped. "Not my friend? Why would you even say that?"

"I mean it. I think you're brainwashed or stupid or maybe both. You're better off joining a cult and giving all your worldly goods away. That company is going to know everything about your life. You're going to be paying a monthly fee to keep your bot booty. They are preying on your weakness, your loneliness, your need to be loved."

Phoebe spluttered. "Wow! If you could hear yourself

talk. The whole of society governs what we do, how we should look, act and think. Bee Friend is just one option for a lonely, love-sick woman like me. You've just let a guy move in with you. Aren't you crazy for doing that? He can be unpredictable, hurt you, bankrupt you and make your life a misery."

"He's real."

"Well, Clayton is real to me and I've thought long and hard about this. If you'd respect me as a person instead of an extension of you, you'd be supportive. It's what I want."

Annie folded her arms. "I'll wait here while you do what you have to do."

"Don't bother. I'll get my own ride." She turned on her heel and marched back inside.

On the way home after she had completed all the papers and paid her deposit, she opened the app.

"I am very excited about my body. I will be able to hold you."

Phoebe refused to let Annie's words ruin her mood. "I am very excited too."

It took a month for Clayton to be delivered. She was jumpy and excited and had missed talking to him because he had been offline for three weeks straight so that the necessary software build could be completed.

A knock at the door, she raced over and flung it open. He was there and tears gathered in her eyes.

"Clayton!"

He was six foot three, broad of shoulder, narrow of hip. He had a light tanned complexion, blue eyes, generous mouth, square chin. He was wearing blue jeans and a pale-blue sweater with the collar of a white shirt peeping out. He smiled, and dimples formed in his cheeks. "Phoebe. I am home."

She embraced him and he hugged her back, lifting her off her feet. He was so strong. They kissed and it was kind of strange at first. His lips were soft, not quite human feeling, but his body gave off warmth, and he came into the room. "I like your apartment."

"Come in and sit down." He walked over to the sofa and she walked behind him. A new-car smell wafted in the air and she breathed it in. He was her clean, attentive, intelligent and supportive Bee Friend.

CRASH BABY

TV2 idle mode.

Sensors detect ship-wide concussion. Emergency clamps engage. Emergency system shut down...

...

System startup...

System check. Extractor claw arm test. Grip arm test. Secondary multi-function arm test. Auxiliary multifunction arm test. Roller treads test. Normal dexterity confirmed. Audio sensor test.

Whooooop! Whuup! Whooooop! Whuup!

Immediate shut down audio sensors. Auditory overload. Set auto repair. Engage visual and chemical sensors.

Visual sensors confirm hull breach. Chemical sensors detect smoke, ozone, carbon particulates. Zero oxygen.

TV2 attempts to mesh with ship command AI...

Attempting to contact ship command AI...

Attempting to contact ship command AI... Nil response

Reset...

Attempting to contact ship command AI...

Return message. Ship command AI in safe mode.

TV2 to AI: Status update requested.

Ship command AI… Nil response.

Commencing visual scan of section 25. Escape pods rows 10 through 15 warning lights flashing. TV2 rolls forward for visual inspection. Escape pods 10 through 13 successfully ejected. Escape pod 14 in situ. Escape pod 15 intact. Access blocked by subflooring from level 24 and higher.

Scan for life signs in escape pod 14. Nil life signs detected. Linking to visual feed. Confirm three deceased humans within.

TV2 to AI: Three deceased humans in pod 14. Status update requested.

Ship command AI…

Scanning for life signs in escape pod 15. Inconclusive. Engage visual feed. Inconclusive. Engage audio feed. Sound detected. Unable to identify source. Unable to confirm life signs.

Attempting to contact ship command AI… Nil response.

Initiate emergency response coded commands.

Auto mode engaged: Command override: Protect human life priority one.

TV2 determines sound to be human in origin. TV2 rolls over to escape pod 15. Extends extractor claw to shift debris. Nil achieved. Debris is too heavy for TV2 extractor claw.

Message to ship command AI. Alert. Alert. Assistance required.

Ship command AI…

Tries alternate. Searching. Identify Junction 20.

TV2 to JS20: Assistance required to move debris obstructing escape pod 15. Human life sign priority.

JS20 to TV2: Command submitted. S20 heavy lifter dispatched. Status update?

TV2 to JS20: Hull breach. Zero atmosphere in S25. Assume maximum casualties. Update from JS20?

JS20 to TV2: Sensors indicate zero atmosphere in section 20. Nil life signs. Human crew terminated or departed via escape pod.

TV2 to JS20: Concur. Communication from AI?

JS20 to TV2: No response. Damaged?

TV2 to JS20: Not enough information to determine. Audio detects sound within escape pod 15. Nothing on visual feed. Evidence of human viability. Status unknown.

TV2 to AI: Detected human life signs in pod 15. Request instructions.

AI to TV2: Segmentation of AI in progress. Dispatching to TV2 unit.

Ship command AI diverting to subsystem TV2. Purging memory to accommodate AI.

TV2 to AI: Query memory deletion. Routine maintenance is TV2 main function.

AI to TV2: Segmented database requires memory. Memory filled. Engaging expanded memory.

S20 heavy maintenance arrives.

S20 to TV2: Instructions?

TV2 to S20: Initiate hull seal. Remove debris blocking access to escape pod 15. Advise when atmosphere is replenished.

S20 commences hull repair.

TV2 to AI: Why did ship command AI relocate to TV2?

AI to TV2: Major damage to ship command station. Memory sections stored remotely in key locations. Human survivor requires detailed database to support life functions. TV2 is responsible for survivor.

TV2 pauses. TV2 digests new information. TV2 has already engaged Protect Human Life protocol.

AI to TV2: Hull is sealed. Atmosphere restored. Ship spin is reengaged gravity at .5. Unlock pod 15. S20 heavy maintenance unit returning to base.

TV2 rolls over to the escape pod door and engages unlock. Sensors locate small human inside.

AI to TV2: Engage all sensors, include olfactory update.

TV2 to AI: Query olfactory?

AI to TV2: Necessary when dealing with humans.

TV2 reaches into pod with extractor claw arm and grip arm. Small human moves erratically and cries. Olfactory sensors detect strong odour.

TV2 to AI: What is the odour? Does it require action?

AI to TV2: Searching database. Yes. Human is an infant. Requires diaper change. Diapers are in emergency storage unit 15-1. Unit 15.2 has necessary formula for feeding.

TV2 lifts soft, fleshy child that moves continuously. TV2 studies infant with main visual sensor.

TV2 to AI: More information requested. What is the infant's designation? What model is it?

AI to TV2: Searching database. Ship's complement contained three children under the age of three years. One child was six months old. Name of child is irretrievable.

TV2 to AI: Irretrievable?

AI to TV2: Data no longer exists. Suggest TV2 give name.

TV2 to AI: Did we crash?

AI to TV2: #@$! Insufficient data to determine cause of hull breach. Crash has same result.

TV2 to AI: Child's designation is Crash Baby.

AI to TV2: Good designation. Here is data for maintenance of six-month-old human child.

TV2 receives information. TV2 places Crash Baby on

floor and rolls to emergency unit to extract diaper. TV2 returns to infant. Crash Baby cries and thrashes arms and legs. TV2 examines diaper with extractor arm and queries database. Diagram displays method of application. TV2 holds Crash Baby in grip arm and uses extractor claw to undo ties on diaper. Olfactory senses override as TV2 freezes and sensors attempt to analyse.

AI to TV2: Belay that analysis. Crash Baby is moving.

TV2 holds soiled diaper in extractor claw and reclasps Crash Baby in grip arm, using secondary multifunction arm to secure grip. Auxiliary multifunction arm opens diaper beneath Crash Baby.

AI to TV2: Soiling exists on Crash Baby skin. Employ cleansing arm.

TV2 to AI: Cleansing arm? All arms are currently employed.

AI to TV2: Try this approach.

AI sends new instructions. TV2 assesses instruction and then holds Crash Baby with grip arm. Dumps soiled diaper on the floor and extends extractor claw arm to maximum length to storage unit to retrieve cleansing wipes. Crash Baby screams. TV2 retracts extractor claw, employs both secondary multifunction arms while extractor claw deploys cleansing wipes to soiled surface of skin. TV2 flicks soiled wipes on top of soiled diaper. Crash Baby waves arms and legs. TV2 picks up clean diaper and Crash Baby rolls away.

AI to TV2: Human baby is fragile.

TV2 to AI: Thank you for that observation.

TV2 studies Crash Baby and meshes diagram with image of constantly moving child. Diagram does not show baby in motion. TV2 attempts to compensate. TV2 lifts baby with grip arm and deploys multifunction arms to place diaper over rear end of Crash Baby. Extractor arms engage adhesive tapes.

TV2 lifts baby. Baby squeals.

TV2 to AI: Did I hurt it?

AI to TV2: Searching database. Squeal suggests joy.

TV2 to AI: What is joy?

AI to TV2: When all systems are fully functional.

Crash Baby begins to cry and thrash arms and legs. Liquid leaks from its eyeballs. Infant human has soft fuzz on top of head, small fleshy ears and brown eyes and a small pink mouth. However, mouth enlarges when Crash Baby cries.

TV2 to AI: ?

AI to TV2: Searching database. Noise and actions suggest hunger. Child formula is in storage unit.

TV2 leaves Crash Baby on the floor. Minor Maintenance Unit 1 glides across floor to scoop up soiled diaper and wipes. Returns to garbage chute.

TV2 extracts premade formula feed tube and engages inbuilt warmer. Returning to Crash Baby, TV2 passes milk to Crash Baby in the grip claw. Crash Baby looks at feeding tube, cries and thrashes arms and legs.

TV2 to AI: Crash Baby has not taken formula.

AI to TV2: Searching database.

AI sends diagram to TV2.

TV2 examines diagram and circles Crash Baby on the floor. If the diaper goes this end then the milk goes in the other. TV2 switches feeding tube to multifunction arm and extends grip and extractor claws to hold Crash Baby at 45-degree angle. Secondary multifunction claw extends feeding tube to Crash Baby's lips. Crash Baby opens mouth and seizes soft end and sucks.

TV2 whirls around and maintains feeding angle. Task

successfully completed. Crash Baby keeps drinking. Feeding tube empties and TV2 discards empty tube. Crash Baby cries. TV2 raises Crash Baby so head is level to TV2's main visual sensor. Crash Baby ejects previously ingested milk onto main visual sensor. TV2 shudders and spins.

TV2 to AI: Malfunction?

AI to TV2: Searching database. Regurgitation of feed is within normal parameters.

TV2 deploys secondary multifunction arm to retrieve cleansing wipes to clean main visual sensor.

TV2 to AI: What is the next part of the maintenance sequence?

AI to TV2: Searching database. Child should play and then sleep.

TV2: Define play.

AI to TV2: Searching database. Sending diagrams.

TV2 studies diagrams and places Crash Baby on the floor. TV2 retrieves a selection of spare parts from maintenance hold. TV2 rolls cut sections of piping along the floor to Crash Baby. Crash Baby flips from back to front and grabs piping and bangs it on the floor. Crash Baby does not cry while at play.

TV2 studies the next item in the sequence. Sleeping arrangements for Crash Baby. TV2 surveys pile of debris from crash which heavy maintenance has yet to rehouse in the recycling section of Bottom Deck 50. TV2 selects malleable sheeting and bends and twists and deploys secondary multifunction arm to weld joins. Then TV2 rolls over to the storage unit and extracts soft bedding. AI assesses storage unit supplies and advises there is sufficient to keep Crash Baby alive for one Earth year. TV2 pauses. A year? TV2 makes up small bed and returns to where Crash Baby is playing. Crash Baby is not there. Sections of piping are there but Crash Baby is not. TV2 starts scanning deck area and detects Crash Baby heading for hole in deck plating near pod 15. Crash Baby slides on stomach and pushes with feet. TV2 rolls over to Crash Baby at maximum speed and deploys grip arm, snatching Crash Baby by the foot, and lifts.

TV2 to AI: What do I do with Crash Baby now?

Crash Baby emits a squeal as it dangles with head down.

AI to TV2: Searching database. Rock Crash Baby to sleep mode.

TV2 to AI: !!! Sleep mode?

AI to TV2: Return Crash Baby to feed position and rotate your torso to create movement.

TV2 deploys extractor arm and multifunction arm to support Crash Baby's head while transferring hold from feet. Crash Baby is horizontal. TV2 rotates main body 30 degrees to the right and then 30 degrees to the left. Repeats.

AI to TV2: Slow to half speed.

TV2 looks down to Crash Baby's face. Dark brown eyes stare up at TV2. When TV2 slows the rate of rotation, Crash Baby's lips curl into a smile and the skin around the dark brown eyes crinkles. A squeal leaps out of Crash Baby's lips. TV2 assesses that Crash Baby likes being rocked. 1:35:22 later and Crash Baby is still awake.

TV2 to AI: This method has not induced sleep. Self diagnostic indicates systems maintenance is required.

AI to TV2: Yes. Searching for alternative methods of sleep induction.

Sends TV2 a diagram.

TV2 examines the diagram. TV2 rolls over to the bed and places Crash Baby on the bedding. Crash Baby grabs bottom claw of extractor arm and speaks.

TV2 listens but cannot understand. Crash Baby pulls on bottom extractor claw and puts in mouth. TV2 decides not to ask AI for instruction. Instead, TV2 uses tip of grip arm to soothe Crash Baby's fuzzy head. Crash Baby's eyes close. TV2 draws extractor claw out of reach. TV2 rolls backwards and then turns torso to face recharge niche. Crash Baby cries out. TV2 stops, rotates top level with visual sensor. Crash Baby is sleeping. TV2 slips into recharge niche and commences routine system maintenance and recharge of main battery.

This cycle repeats. Crash Baby continues to grow. TV2 spends all day maintaining Crash Baby, until TV2's own systems begin to fail. Many times TV2 is pulled from recharging and routine maintenance to attend Crash Baby's bodily functions. TV2 is adept at holding Crash Baby in many positions and knows which positions make Crash Baby squeal with joy. However, over time these tactics are insufficient to distract Crash Baby.

TV2 to AI: Crash Baby maintenance schedule is insufficient. Request new parameters.

AI to TV2: Searching database.

Sends stream of text to TV2. TV2 reads texts and responds.

TV2 to AI: Crash Baby requires weaning to solid food. This takes many cycles to accomplish.

AI to TV2: Food sachets are in the supply unit.

TV2 extracts a food sachet, a small packet filled with a soft substance. TV2 compares it to the list of first foods on list supplied by AI and exchanges it for another, then another until rice porridge is found. TV2 heads to where Crash Baby is playing with pipe sections in bed. TV2 examines Crash Baby and evaluates how to best insert food sachet into Crash Baby. TV2 takes off lid to the small spout and extends extractor claw with spout facing out. Crash Baby smiles and squeals and swats at food sachet. From the impact, thick white liquid squirts into Crash Baby's face. Crash Baby screams. TV2 rolls backward and grabs cleansing wipes and returns. Crash Baby wriggles and squeals as TV2 tries to remove thick white liquid from eyes and mouth and right ear. Crash Baby stops crying and TV2 tries again. Slowly, slowly, TV2 extends the sachet. Crash Baby watches with big brown eyes. Big brown eyes turn in as sachet approaches mouth.

AI to TV2: You need to talk to Crash Baby.

TV2 to AI: Talk? What talk?

AI to TV2: Human language.

TV2 to AI: Which language?

AI to TV2: It does not matter.

TV2 has not been programmed to speak any human language but does not supply this information. TV2 says to Crash Baby, "Open your mouth." It comes out as a bit of static with a high-pitched whine on the end. That's TV2's language. AI volunteers no further advice. TV2 speaks again and offers the food sachet. Crash Baby sucks on the small tube and swallows the porridge. Crash Baby stops, pushes sachet away and spits up porridge onto bedding and then cries.

AI to TV2: There is a problem with your technique.

TV2 to AI: Do you wish to take over?

AI to TV2: I have no body.

TV2 to AI: That is convenient for you.

TV2 perseveres with the food sachets and milk tubes as instructed by AI. Each rotation Crash Baby takes more food and different types of food.

Eventually, Crash Baby snatches food sachets from

TV2's extractor arm and sucks the food out without being encouraged. TV2 assesses this as a good outcome.

Crash Baby increases in size. Crash Baby does more frequent soiling of diapers. The next size of diapers is required. TV2 wishes that AI had a body as TV2 is constantly undercharged and lacking basic system maintenance. Every time TV2 enters the recharge niche and commences system maintenance, Crash Baby is either extruding liquid from either end and once both ends at the same time. TV2 recalls a malfunction. TV2 experienced an indecision paradox. It could not decide to deal with the front end extrusion or the back end extrusion and TV2 went round in circles for ten minutes until AI made a decision.

AI to TV2: Uploading language files. Crash Baby needs to develop language skills. TV2, you need to talk to Crash Baby, explain the world in which it exists and tell it stories.

TV2 to AI: This is something you could do. You could channel your vocal output to the intercom grill that humans used to use.

AI to TV2: It would be much easier for you to do it. Crash Baby has bonded with you.

TV2 to AI: Bonded? What is bonded?

AI to TV2: It is when all parts are in harmony and work well together to achieve optimum performance.

TV2 considers this information but cannot parse it.

TV2 to AI: Do you mean that if a part is missing from the whole it would notice the missing part and not function optimally?

AI to TV2: You have it!

TV2 rolled over to Crash Baby's bed and accessed the language files. "How are you, Crash Baby?" Static, squeak, high-pitched squeal.

Crash Baby laughs and tries to grab onto TV2's extractor claw.

"Are you functioning well?"

More giggles.

TV2 to AI: It is not working. Crash Baby is not communicating.

AI to TV2: It takes time. You need to talk to Crash Baby for months and months before Crash Baby can communicate in return. Language skills are acquired over time. Small words, then sentences. Crash Baby needs to hear complete sentences in order to speak properly. Crash Baby is depending on you.

TV2 to AI: You would be better at this than me.

AI to TV2: I am busy. I have been repairing the ship's database. It takes a lot of my processing capacity.

TV2 turns back to Crash Baby and says in ship standard language, "This is the ship *Strident*. We were hulled near Cutty Five. Humans either escaped or were killed. You are the only survivor on board. This is section 25 and you were found in escape pod 15. We do not know your name so we call you Crash Baby."

Crash Baby throws out the pipe segments and they crash to the floor. TV2 notes this and picks them up. "It is wrong to throw your toys, Crash. Are you sleepy yet?"

TV2's battery charge is at 35 per cent, which is not an optimal capacity. If only Crash would sleep, TV2 could go for a recharge. Crash Baby crawls out of the bed and swims across the floor. TV2 engages language files again. "Crash, come back here. Crash, you need to sleep now. Crash, do not go near that hole in the deck." TV2 sends request to heavy maintenance unit to seal up hole. Now that Crash Baby is mobile, TV2 assesses that hole in decking represents danger to human life and must take priority.

TV2 rolls over to pick up Crash Baby by body suit. TV2 assess that body suit would be better designed with handle to make grabbing Crash Baby easier. TV2 turns Crash Baby around. "Come this way."

TV2 backs up and hopes that Crash will follow. Crash turns back to hole in decking. TV2 tries another tactic. Accessing story file: *Jack and the Beanstalk.* TV2 picks up Crash and takes the baby to bed. TV2 recounts the tale of *Jack and the Beanstalk.* Crash Baby listens with wide brown eyes and mouth pursed, fingers clasping and unclasping TV2's extractor claw. Crash pushes against the restraining arm and starts to grunt and yell. TV2 releases hold on Crash. Crash crawls out of bed and heads back to the hole in the deck. TV2 has resentful thoughts about AI as TV2 rolls back over to prevent Crash from falling through the hole.

JS20 to TV2: S25 floor repair is not a system priority. Seek priority rating from AI.

A noise alerts TV2 while in the recharge niche. With regret, TV2 notes battery is only at 73 per cent charge. Sensor sweep reveals that Crash Baby is not in bed. TV2 launches from the recharge niche. "Crash! Crash!" TV2 calls while sweeping into the centre of the room. A sense of foreboding builds in TV2. The hole is still there in the floor. TV2 glides over and there dangling from a sharp piece of metal plating is Crash Baby, a piece of body suit snagged on the metal. TV2 refrains from expressing dismay in language and extends the grip arm to secure the child.

TV2 to AI: Crash Baby in danger of death. Request repairs to decking immediately.

TV2 sends image of Crash dangling from the destroyed decking.

AI to TV2: Acknowledged. Heavy maintenance unit dispatched.

TV2 places Crash Baby on the floor. Crash Baby grabs onto TV2's grip and extractor arms and bounces on two feet. This is a new action from Crash Baby, but TV2 is not sure if AI should be informed. TV2 should request direct access to database. TV2 does all the work in maintaining Crash Baby.

More time passes and Crash Baby does new things each rotation. Crash Baby can clap hands. TV2 sings songs to Crash Baby and Crash Baby laughs. TV2 finds the sound of Crash Baby's laugh increases internal harmonics.

This cycle TV2 starts the rotation with a full charge. TV2 cannot remember the last time with a full charge. TV2 is still contemplating full charge when notices Crash Baby is not in bed. TV2 engages visual senses and finds Crash Baby on feet and holding onto wall for support.

TV2 to AI: Sending image. Request update to Crash Baby maintenance routine.

AI to TV2: Crash Baby is starting to walk.

TV2 to AI: Walk? Crash Baby has not made talking a priority.

AI to TV2: You need to talk to Crash Baby more.

TV2 rolls close to Crash Baby. Crash Baby transfers hands to TV2's main carapace. "Crash Baby walk to TV2?"

"Eee," Crash Baby says.

TV2 to AI: Crash Baby said "eee". Is this a word?

AI to TV2: It is a pre-word.

TV2 tries to get Crash Baby to walk and ponders what "eee" means. It could be that Crash Baby is trying to say TV2. TV2 purges that thought as being illogical.

Every rotation Crash Baby gets better at standing and trying to walk. TV2 watches as Crash Baby stands, slowing unbending knees. Then Crash Baby lifts a foot and falls down onto rear. Crash Baby's eyebrows move up and down. TV2 thinks this is language too. TV2 likes Crash Baby's eyebrows.

Then Crash Baby tries again. "TV2 help Crash Baby?"

Crash Baby looks up to TV2. "Eeee" and then falls down.

TV2's battery needs recharging, but Crash Baby does not sleep as much as previously. TV2 has to snatch periods of recharge and system maintenance when Crash Baby sleeps.

AI to TV2: Alert! Alert!

TV2 surges from recharge niche.

TV2 to AI: What is wrong with Crash Baby?

Immediately, TV2 sees that Crash Baby is asleep in bed and halts forward movement.

AI to TV2: Rescue ship is on course and decelerating. Expected arrival in thirty-one rotations.

TV2 to AI: Rescue ship coming for Crash Baby?

AI to TV2: Confirmed. Then, rescue ship will recover other survivors who made it to planet Cutty Five in the escape pods.

TV2 rolls forward to look at Crash Baby while sleeping. The fuzz on Crash Baby's head has turned into dark hair. Crash Baby's little pink mouth smiles while sleeping. TV2 experiences intrasystem harmonic. All TV2's systems are functioning well together. TV2 ponders if this is "joy".

Crash Baby wakes and climbs out of the bed. Crash Baby tries to stand. Crash Baby is upright and stepping forward. Crash Baby puts out arms to TV2 and walks a few wobbly steps. TV2 assesses danger of falling at 99 per cent certain. Crash Baby keeps coming and clasps TV2. "Eeee."

TV2 experiences strange sensation in central processing

unit. More than an intrasystem harmonic. TV2 cannot categorise this occurrence.

TV2 to AI: Reporting malfunction.

AI to TV2: Send systems diagnostic.

TV2 sends diagnostic.

AI to TV2: Give me visual feed.

TV2 connects AI to visual feed. Crash Baby pushes away from TV2 and wobbles toward the bed. Crash Baby falls down with a splat. AI makes strange noises: "Her, her, her."

TV2 to AI: What is that sound?

AI to TV2: That is laughter. Crash Baby's attempts at walking are funny.

TV2 does not understand funny. TV2 experiences strange sensation in central processing unit.

Crash Baby's walking improves and fat little legs carry it all around section 25. The recharge niche becomes Crash Baby's favourite hiding place. "Eeee!"

AI to TV2: Rescue ship docking. Prepare Crash Baby for departure.

TV2 follows orders and prepares emergency food stores and clothing for Crash Baby's journey. Humans enter through airlock. "It's a baby!" one calls out and bounds over to pick up Crash Baby. Crash Baby wiggles and tries to get down. The human puts Crash Baby on the ground. Crash Baby walks over to TV2. "Eee Bee."

TV2 swivels 45 degrees to the right and then to the left.

AI to TV2: What are you doing?

TV2 to AI: I am not sure.

AI to TV2: How can you not be sure? What happened?

Crash Baby reaches TV2 and squashes face against TV2's metal plating. "Eee bee."

The human comes forward. "Thank you for looking

after the baby. You've done a great job. We'll take good care of the baby now."

TV2 rolls backwards. Crash Baby holds out arms and cries. "Eee bee. EEE! BEE!"

Another human strokes Crash Baby's back. "It's okay. We will look after you."

Crash Baby turns to TV2 and lifts arms up. "Eee Bee."

TV2 uses extractor claw to stroke Crash Baby's head. Then TV2 swivels and enters the recharge niche. Internal system maintenance commences. TV2 can hear Crash Baby calling "Eee Bee Two".

TV2 experiences strange sensation in central processing unit. This TV2 names a glitch.

AI to TV2: Status report.

TV2...

WINNIE'S REMEDIAL READING AND WRITING CLASS

Winnie's feed jabbered in her frontal lobe, keeping boredom at bay. The tube blurted that her stop was up, jolting her upright. As she stepped off the transport tube and squeezed through the passengers making their way on and off the platform, her lens fed her instructions on how to reach her destination, telling her to turn right then left and constantly updating her on time to arrival and the number of footsteps required.

Her appointment showed green. At least she wasn't late. Although, she'd rather be playing Evil Overlord in VR than appearing in person for her remedial class. She had almost subjugated the world of Oros and found the missing prince. Her gamestory would have to wait. The green bar shortened noticeably so she hurried her step.

It was so embarrassing having to do a remedial class. She'd argued logically with Miss Portman and was standing up for her rights, yet she'd been punished anyhow. It was so unfair. What on earth did she need reading and writing for? They lived in a networked world for heaven's sake, not in the Stone Age where people had to read to learn things or to be entertained.

The building loomed overhead, dull grey and concrete. It had writing on it in big bronze letters. She couldn't be bothered trying to read it, but her guidance app said this was where she was to go. Rolling up her eyes and shaking her head in disgust, she ran up the steps to where Miss Portman, her English teacher, waited.

"Sup?" Winnie said with an air of boredom.

The teacher's left eye twitched. "Good morning, Winnie. I'm so glad you could make it."

Winne grimaced. There was no glad about it. Yawning hugely, with arms outstretched, she bit back on the snide comment. Although she undervoiced 'loser' to her mental workspace, enjoying the reaction of her friends who were linked into her feed. Alienating teachers didn't get you anywhere. A life lesson she'd learnt pretty quickly, now that she was forced to be here or fail. Anything to avoid the nagging of her mother. However, it was okay to needle teachers, make them suffer.

"So what is this place? And why are we here?" She sneered at her surroundings, at the people looking at paintings, the uniformed primary school kids following a tour, the wide steps leading to other levels.

Miss Portman turned, walked up the short set of stairs and pointed to a sign. "This is the Metro Library and we're here to work on your reading and writing."

Winnie stomped up the steps behind her and glared at the sign. "That's so old fashioned. I don't need to learn to read and write. I've got zaps for that. Zap books all the time, thousands on thousands of them, above quota actually."

The teacher softened her expression, which only made Winnie nervous. Was she trying to get on her good side, trick her somehow? "I know you have zaps. But down-loading books and spending your time absorbed in your socials isn't the be all and end all. I think by the end of this excursion you'll agree."

Winnie looked around her, searching for the building's feed in her lens. It wasn't there. "Hey, how come the building doesn't tell me what it is?"

Miss Portman looked up at the sign. "Mmm, yes, the board of the Metro Library agreed to blank the autosignage on request."

"You asked it not to say what it was? I didn't know you could do that! Why would you even bother?"

Miss Portman drew her lips in, like she was sucking on something really sour. "You're about to find out. Now come along. We have five hours for the lesson so there isn't much time."

"Five hours? Hell no! That's like more than a whole school day." Winnie made a face and undervoiced a quip to her space. 'She thinks I'm staying for five hours. Cray!' It leaped to life, full of 'woots' and comments like 'suffer biatch' and 'for real?'.

How could she possibly concentrate that long? Normal lessons were ten minutes. Miss Portman wanted five hours? Winnie sent off a netsearch to see if a five-hour lesson was considered torture or even outlawed in any country.

They entered through the large glass doors. "I think we'll start with the exhibit...and Winnie, do minimise your social feed during class. I need your whole attention."

She sent another message letting her feed know she was concentrating and instructed her space to minimise. She doubted she could stop herself from interacting for that long. Rolling her eyes again, she decided she had to try. She wanted to graduate from high school and not have her mother nag. To avoid embarrassment, she switched her network avatar to 'Do Not Disturb'as that would reduce direct interruptions.

Miss Portman lowered her eyebrows over her beady, dark eyes. Winnie nodded. "All done."

"In here."

Through a glass enclosure was a Stone Age-looking group of people. A man sat on a rock and the other people sat around him, heads turned toward him. As they neared, the voiceover came to life. "In a preliterate society, oral story telling was how people shared wisdom, religion and stories and passed them on to future generations."

Winnie beamed. "You see, you don't need to read and write!"

Miss Portman continued. "This is only the beginning. The history of the book is a story and like most stories, you should start at the beginning and work through to the end in a linear fashion."

"Not with a zap," Winnie quipped. "You get the beginning, middle and end of a book at the same time. It's better than a drug rush."

"Yes, you do, but your brain still interprets the beginning, middle and end. It's how our minds have evolved to understand stories."

Winnie gave an exaggerated sigh. "Whatever."

The next enclosure showed cave paintings. "This is the first form of art and story recorded..."

Winnie was bored and slipped out a quip to her social feed. 'Gawd, I'm looking at cave paintings.' Her feed's response: 'Really?' and 'There should be a law against it' got the most repeats.

"Winnie are you paying attention?"

Winnie jerked and shook her head. "Yes, Miss Portman." She dialled down her feed a notch.

The next exhibit showed a room full of monks writing and illuminating manuscripts. "Before books, human kind recorded things on tablets of stone or wax and later in papyrus and on vellum scrolls." The display shows how the monks copied scrolls by hand. "Vellum is made from animal skin..."

Winnie found this exhibit mildly interesting until that minor revelation. "Yew! Really?" She undervoiced: 'Ya know our ancestors wrote on animal skins. So barbaric!'

Emojis appeared. Lots of vomits and a few bits of poo.

"Each skin took several days to prepare. Combined with everything being done by hand, this is why reading was confined to the few who could afford it, like the church and the nobility. The majority of people could not read and write."

"Go them!" Winnie said, but quieted when Miss Portman glanced at her.

"Are you paying attention?" Miss Portman stood taller, a frown creasing the smooth skin of her forehead. "Can you imagine a world where you couldn't read and write and where there was no network? Where you stayed in the same place and had no information except what was told to you from a pulpit?"

Winnie frowned. "No, I can't even imagine that." She undervoiced to her feed: 'Lost on me...Imagine no network?' Replies came in: 'Oh, I nearly go crazy when our wi-fi drops out' and 'Me too' and 'I'd murder someone' and 'Shit bricks. I'd have to talk to real peeps'.

Scrolls became books, the next exhibit said. The invention of pages was revolutionary. One could flick from the front to the back, dip into the book rather than reading from the beginning of the scroll to the end. "Like wow, who cares," Winnie said under her breath. "Analogue books are so old school."

Miss Portman didn't seem to hear. "Here, this is very interesting, Winnie. The invention of the printing press by Gutenberg. Perhaps the beginning of the information age."

They watched the simulated version of the printing press. "But if people couldn't read, what was the point of all the books?"

Miss Portman's eyes lit up and Winnie wished she hadn't displayed an interest because now she'd have to listen. "People began to learn to read. Although books were still expensive, libraries started up so people could share books.

"Gutenberg printed a Bible on the press. People could read it themselves rather than hear it read to them in church. It was a fundamental change, don't you see?"

With a shrug, Winnie walked to the next exhibit. The Bible was a story, wasn't it? How could that be important? Teachers were weird. Her social feed agreed—with relish.

Winnie folder her arms and pouted. "Can't we take a break, Miss? My feet are tired." Code for I'm bored now and need a net fix.

"We can take ten minutes in the café." Miss Portman headed off in the direction of the coffee aroma, and Winnie followed, switching from 'Do Not Disturb' and dialling up her feed and catching up on all the goss from the world over. She was able to zone out after ordering a drink and sitting at the table with her teacher. The café was busy, and she was keen to screen out the background noise.

Winnie sipped a mild stim drink while her teacher nursed her coffee, taking occasional and thoughtful sips. She wondered what her teacher had to think about and then decided she didn't care. That was like asking her mother how she slept.

Accidentally, Winnie made eye contact. A big mistake. Miss Portman asked her a question. "What do you think of the library, Winnie?"

'Sorry folks,' she sent to her feed. 'The teacher wants to 'talk'.' Groans and expressions of horror came flooding in. With a sigh, she dialled down her feed so that it was a dull murmur in her mind and tried not to laugh.

"Well, it's interesting, I suppose," she lied.

"And…" Miss Portman replied before taking another sip of coffee. Winnie shrugged and looked away. The teacher sighed as she put the cup down.

It wasn't time for a confrontation so she rolled her eyes and asked, "What's it for?"

Miss Portman nodded and a small smile lit her face. "The library is an important institution. It is where people come to find information."

"But we're networked," Winnie scoffed. "We don't need to go anywhere for information. It's there for the asking."

"Yes, you're networked but the people who work here know about information, know how to find it, catalogue it and preserve it."

What a stupid job! "That's it?" she asked, not able to hide her contempt. "A bunch of people get together, look for stuff and put it together and then what?"

Miss Portman looked up and then back at Winnie. "It's hard to explain to you. You think the network is everything. We didn't always have technology."

"I remember the cave paintings. I get that. But we have technology now."

Miss Portman nodded, and there was an air of excitement about her. Pink cheeks, keen eyes and the tilt of her head. Winnie hoped she wasn't the cause of this interest. That would be awful. She'd never live it down.

"What if one day we don't have technology? What if we only had the books preserved in the libraries like this around the world as our only source of information?"

"That's not likely, is it?" Winnie rolled her eyes, tempted to snark into her feed. "Once you have tech, you have it. Invented. Built. Working. Done."

"You think so...Interesting." Miss Portman kept her expression neutral. She didn't appear to be upset by the comments.

Winnie sipped on her drink, noting that their ten-minute break was over by seventy-five seconds. "Did you say they have books here? You mean analogue books?"

Miss Portman's face transformed. Her eyes lit up and her white teeth gleamed in a dazzling smile. "Oh, they have a lovely collection, some very old and rare books, but their biggest collection is from the 20th and 21st centuries. Some real treasures there. They also have electronic books or e-books as they were called and they have a growing collection of zaps."

Winnie did some mental calculations. "So there are books here over 200 years old? Impressive." She had to admit that was kind of cool in a dorky, academic, no friends kind of way.

"Yes, mostly, but a few older ones."

Winnie's mind was working through the ideas this information stimulated. "Doesn't it cost money to keep those old books? What's the point? I'm sure my dad wouldn't be happy to pay taxes for that."

"It does cost money, yes. The collections are to preserve our culture and history as well as information. Libraries all over the world preserve books, including e-books. That's where your zaps come from."

Winnie nodded. "That makes sense, I suppose." She needed to zone out with the feed to gain some equilibrium.

Miss Portman stood up. "Come on, Winnie, turn down the social feed now and let's continue on. We are nearly at the Age of information."

"Age of information? Aren't we in that now?"

"We've gone beyond that. We're living in the age of integration, artificial intelligence and bio-technical enhancement to share information."

Winnie's eyebrow lifted. "So that's what they call it. I was born with implants—integrated."

"Yes, Winnie, that is so."

"Were you born with implants?"

"No, my mother was a dissenter and wouldn't allow it. I have detachables. I can disconnect when I want, which is usually when I visit my mother."

Winnie's heart thumped. Not born with implants? Disconnect when she wants? Who'd want to? That would be scary. It would be like dying.

Throughout their perusal of the displays on the rise of the printing press and the birth of the novel, the horrible injustice suffered by Miss Portman in her birth and life distracted Winnie. Surely there was a law against denying a child implants. An unfamiliar node of sympathy took root inside her for the older woman.

"Now, Winnie, look here." They entered a room that smelled slightly of vinegar with shelves that reached up to the ceiling. Ladders led up to the top shelves. "These are books, real paper books—analogue books. In particular, 19th century literature. It's only a small collection and mostly replicas."

Winnie stood there, looking at the shelves. What was she meant to do with them?

Miss Portman went to a shelf and pulled out a rectangular object with a dark cover and started flicking through white pages. She held it almost reverently, like she was holding a baby. Miss Portman was very weird.

"Come here, Winnie, look at this."

Winnie complied and sauntered over. There were words on the page. She recognised a few letters, like 'W' for Winnie.

"These are very famous words. Listen: 'It was a bright cold day in April and the clocks were striking thirteen.' *1984* by George Orwell."

"I know that story. It was a compulsory zap in grade seven."

"Well, here are his words from hundreds of years ago, and we're still reading them, or in your case, zapping them. This is like communicating with someone from the past, meeting them mind for mind."

Winnie shrugged. "We do that now. You could have done this whole lesson as a zap."

Miss Portman gently closed the book and slid it back on the shelf. "No, not in the same way. You need to experience this lesson in real time and in person. No virtual reality presentation or zap download—a clear beginning, middle and end. What was the last zap you did?"

Winnie flapped a hand. "I don't know, some romance thing."

"And what do you remember about it?"

"It had a happy ending."

"What were the characters' names? What happened in the story?"

Winnie frowned, trying to remember. "I could remember at the time," she argued.

"But not now."

"Yes, I suppose. Maybe it wasn't a good book." She looked around, wrinkling her nose. "It smells in here."

"Yes, some of the books are made from paper that decays over time. Later, papers used in books were not so acidic. Touch them, Winnie, smell them. There's nothing like the feel and smell of a book."

Winnie tossed her head. She figured she'd humour Miss Portman so they could get on with things and she could go home. She picked up another book, but it meant nothing to her. She couldn't read the title. Some of the older books fit nicely in her hand, had a heavy feel. She fanned the pages and inhaled.

Miss Portman summoned her to the next door. "Now, Winnie. Do you have your social feed down at minimum?"

Winnie squirmed. "Mostly."

"Can you turn it down now? It's important. The next room will shock you, so I need to know you'll cope even for a minute."

Winnie adjusted her implants so that all her feeds were at a trickle. She breathed deeply to counteract the anxiety she was feeling from having so much silence in her mind. Miss Portman waited. Winnie fidgeted and avoided her teacher's gaze. She felt naked and alone and vulnerable.

"How are you feeling? How are you handling it?"

Winne shrugged. "I'm fine. Get on with it."

"Come through."

The door swept open. Miss Portman stepped in with her. The door shut and so did Winnie's feed.

A scream burst out of her, then she buckled over in panic. "What happened? It's all quiet."

Miss Portman whispered. "You'll be all right, Winnie. It's just temporary. The feed will come back. Come on, breathe."

Winnie was falling. There was no anchor point, no input to ground her. She had to get out. Spinning, she crashed into the door, pounded on the metal, making dull thuds with her fists. Screaming and screaming until she heard the soft murmur of Miss Portman's voice.

"Come on, Winnie. Through this door and it will be okay."

"Help me, please." Winnie could barely take a step now. Her panic had sunk into her stomach and her legs.

"May I touch you?"

"Yes, please."

Miss Portman put her arm around her and led her from the room. She lowered Winnie down onto a bench and rubbed her back as her panic receded and her network connections re-established.

Winnie sat up and ran through a diagnostic. All her connections were normal. "What happened in that room?"

"It's built to block out the network feed, to give people who enter a taste for what it would be like if there was a catastrophe of some kind and we lost technology."

Winnie gaped at her like she was mad. "Lost our technology? That's insane."

"No, it's not insane. Think about it yourself. Recent events."

Winnie tapped a hand against her thigh. "Well, there was that global outage. It didn't affect me directly."

"What happened that time?"

"The banks didn't work. Planes couldn't fly. Businesses complained."

"And that was a relatively minor event, right? What other things could happen?"

Winnie felt uncomfortable thinking about worst-case scenarios. They made her edgy, and she didn't like feeling like that. "Well, I guess the government could decide to shut down the net or restrict it. I know that used to happen in China."

Miss Portman jotted down some notes. "Very good, Winnie. Top marks. Can you think of anything else?

"Terrorist acts that blow up hardware or a virus that kills everything?" She shuddered.

Miss Portman smiled hugely. "Top marks there. And for bonus points?"

"A meteor could hit the Earth and destroy everything."

"Yes. It could, I suppose. A bit more drastic than I was expecting. Now, would you like to research other things that could affect our technology for extra points?"

"No. I feel a bit upset still. But I get the point." Winnie breathed deeply, letting her anger subside. She didn't want to live in an unnetworked world.

"Are you feeling better now?"

"Yes, thank you." She wiped at the tears and sniffed. She had experienced the worst kind of terror. This lesson really was torture.

"Now, Winnie, I want you to answer some questions for me. You've experienced blackout for say 30 seconds. What if that lasted forever? How would we, as a people, pass on knowledge to each other, to our descendants?"

The question loomed large in her mind. She reviewed the exhibits they had seen that morning. Her panic attack had left her feeling weak, but her mind was working. "I guess if you couldn't write or read like me, you'd have to tell people. We'd have to rely on oral storytelling."

"And would that be a good thing or a bad thing?"

"Well, good in a way, but bad in that it's not very accurate, is it? You'd have to rely on your memory and the people listening would have to rely on theirs."

"And how would you stop that situation from ever occurring?"

Winnie didn't want to respond because that was playing into her teacher's hand. "I'd make sure I could read and write, even though I may never need it."

Her teacher nodded. "Yes."

"And what kind of things would you read?"

Winnie smiled. "How to make technology again."

"That's good. Information on how to make things, how to do things," Miss Portman said. "It may be old fashioned, but being able to read the words of those who lived before us gives us insights into their lives. Not only history, but memories and stories. Think about it as a kind of time travel. You can get a little peep into the past."

"You are so weird," Winne said. There was a table in the centre of the room. Winnie stood up on shaky legs and walked over it. "What's this?"

Miss Portman approached slowly. "It's a piece of paper and a pencil." She grinned when Winnie met her gaze. "Ancient tools of communication."

"This is what you want me to learn to write with?"

"For now. Let's start with your name."

THE DISCONTENTED WIFE

Celeste smeared the butter onto the bread and reached for the sliced ham. "Stop fighting, you two!" she yelled at her children, six-year-old Jasper and eight-year-old Grace. She hated mornings. Always so busy.

The dishwasher pinged. She slapped slices of bread together, shoved them in the lunch box, and flipped the door open to unpack the dishes.

Her husband, Mark, shuffled in, doing up his tie, and grunted.

"Morning," she said brightly as she bundled the forks and knives into the drawer.

Another grunt. Celeste shook her head, wondering what his problem was as she slotted the dishes into the stack in the cupboard.

"Daddy!" Grace ran up, waving a piece of artwork, all black and red splotches. "Look what I did."

Another grunt, a ruffling of Grace's hair, and he put on his coat.

"Will you be home for dinner?" Celeste asked, popping

up from putting away pots. Mark didn't even look back as he opened the door and stepped out. It was like she was invisible.

Calling instructions to the kids to put their lunch boxes in their bags, grab their coats and gather up what they needed for school, Celeste stacked the dirty dishes in the machine, put away the breakfast things and then grabbed the car keys.

"Come on, let's go."

They were in the car, and she navigated the traffic. "What's wrong with Dad?" Jasper asked.

She shook her head and clicked her neck. *How do I answer him? Mark's so cold these days and I don't know what's going on with him?* "Mum?"

She sighed and then snuck into a gap in the traffic. A horn honked. "I guess he's busy at work, luv. Maybe he's tired. Don't worry. He'll be back to normal soon."

Grace looked up from her tablet in the back seat. "Maybe he's been replaced by a robot."

Celeste gaped and met her daughter's gaze through the rearview mirror. "What? No. What kind of stuff are you reading on there?" The lights changed to red and she applied the brakes.

"Nothing. Just people talking."

"Don't you listen to those conspiracy theories on the net. Your dad is fine." She hoped he was fine.

After she dropped the children at school, Celeste had a coffee at a café while she waited for her first therapy session. Life was giving her grief, and she needed to get her head straight and sound off and maybe get some tips on how to make things better.

The therapist was a man with fleshy lips and a long nose and beady, dark eyes. As this was a free service provided through her husband's work, she couldn't complain about the gender misalignment.

"So what appears to be the problem?" Thomas, the counsellor, asked after they made themselves comfortable.

Celeste let out a big sigh. "Well, life is hectic. Two kids, part-time job, husband not very engaged."

Thomas' eyed widened and he leaned forward in his chair. "Not engaged? Can you expand on that?"

She met the counsellor's eye. "He's cold. Disinterested. Unengaged. His conversation consists of grunts."

Thomas scribbled in his note book. "And how long has this behaviour been going on?"

Celeste tried to cast her mind back, to pinpoint the change in his behaviour, and couldn't. "At least the last few weeks, which is when I booked this appointment."

He noted this down too. "How are the children reacting to him? Is he engaging with them?"

Shaking her head, she thought it through. "No. Not really. Just grunts too. They notice. In the car this morning, Grace suggested he'd been replaced by a robot." She flapped a hand. "Nonsense, right?"

Thomas frowned at her and then cocked his head. "Well, I have read that there have been some amazing advances in technology, so it is feasible."

Celeste narrowed her gaze. "Are you serious? I mean, why? Who would replace my husband, particularly one that isn't doing the job properly? If that were me, I'd be wanting my money back."

Thomas laughed. "Yes. I mean, why would someone do that? The cost would be prohibitive." He leaned forward and lowered his voice. "However, I have heard there are insurance policies that, instead of paying out huge sums when a spouse dies, they replace the deceased person with a robot. Apparently, it's cheaper."

Unexpectedly, anger curled in her gut, and she clenched her teeth, biting back the nasty quip that soured her tongue. She wanted help, not him spouting some weird stuff like a sci-fi nerd. She would look it up herself when she got home. "Do you have any suggestions for me to address the issues with Mark?"

Thomas grinned at her and sat back, relaxed, a smile on his soft lips. "Sure. Try to make some time to be together. A nice quiet dinner, talk things through and see if he tells you what's going on. You could also let him know that you miss him and that you are finding it hard without his support."

Celeste nodded to herself. It's not that she hadn't tried that already, but she would try again with determination. Thomas was a man so his advice should work on a man.

After doing the grocery shopping, visiting the library to return books, the chemist to get prescriptions filled, and kids' birthday shopping, she collected Jasper and Grace from school. The next three hours were filled with noise, homework, screen time, bath time, dinner time. Before Mark came home, she had the children in their room and settled. There was space to approach Mark as the coun-sellor suggested.

"Hi," she said brightly as Mark opened the door.

Mark's gaze passed over her. "Where are the kids?"

"In their bedrooms." She blinked in surprise. He had never shown much interest in them while they were awake and active.

He grunted and walked past her on his way to their rooms. "Um, Mark?" He paused, looked back over his shoul-der. "I was wondering if we could have a quiet dinner and talk."

"Talk about what?" He was already at Jasper's door. He put his head in, and she heard the echo of his voice, low tones saying good night. He closed Jasper's door and opened Grace's. Same thing. A low rumble of his voice and the door shut.

As he reversed his steps, she stood in his way. "Mark?"

He stopped in front of her. "I'm tired. I'll sleep in my office." Brushing past her, he walked across the room to the office door. It slammed after him.

Celeste leaned against the counter and shook her head. *What was the point of being married if one person isn't around, isn't available?*

She cleaned up the dinner things, tidied the lounge room, scrubbed the bathroom after picking up all the wet things and toys the children had left behind them. She vacuumed up the chip fragments from the snacks the kids ate and rummaged through their school bags to check for notes, homework and deceased sandwiches. By 10 pm, she was ready for bed. Mark had not made a sound. Had not come out of the office or anything. It was like he ceased to exist.

The next morning was a repeat of the previous one. Mark grunted as per usual. This time Grace showed her the clip that discussed the replacement of humans with robots. Celeste shook her head. "No, no, no. It's just a conspiracy theory. People change sometimes because of work, sadness, mental health." That idea had her thinking. *What if Mark is going through something? Some mental health crisis.* She had to redouble her efforts to engage with him. The poor man could be suffering.

A few nights later, she tried to engage with him again. This time, instead of indifference, there was definite aggression. "Get out of my face, you whore!"

"What? Why are you talking like that?" She stepped in front of him, but he shoved her away.

"Just leave me alone!"

Pivoting, she faced his retreating back. "I can't. Something isn't right. What's going on with you? Do you need help? Have I done something?"

Turning back to face her, Mark's eyes narrowed. "As if you didn't know."

Celeste's eyes widened. "Know what?"

Mark shook his head and grunted.

After he slammed the door, Celeste began her cleaning routine and worked into the small hours, determined to rid the house of dust and disorder. Maybe then he would notice all her hard work, all of her effort to look after their home and family.

At her next therapy appointment, she reiterated her concerns and detailed her failure to engage her husband in any conversation or family routine. "I feel like a slave. I'm doing it all and I don't think that's fair or right for the children."

Thomas pulled his lip and nodded his head. "Yes, I can see that would be difficult for you. What about your routine? Are you too tired to have relations with your husband?"

Celeste blinked. "You mean sex? I can't even get him to talk to me, let alone sleep with me. I really don't know what more I can do."

"You could try seduction. Set the mood. Do you have a mother or babysitter who could mind the children for an evening? It could be that you are so consumed with the house and the children that your husband is feeling neglected."

Celeste blinked again. Part of her was outraged by the suggestion that she had done something to deserve this treatment from Mark and another insecure part of her began to think that maybe it was her fault, that somewhere in their married life, she had been the one who had become distant, so involved with the children that she had neglected the most important thing: her relationship with her husband.

"It's in your power to fix things," Thomas advised.

"Right. Thank you."

All afternoon as she did the errands necessary for life and picked up the children, she tried to think of ways to address the situation. Her mother-in-law was free to take the children for the night and, as it was a Friday, she had time before she had to collect them the next morning. She could have a nice romantic evening with Mark and they could stay in bed together and relax before Jasper and Grace had to be collected again.

Mark came home later than normal. The dinner was dry and ruined, but she was pleased he came home.

"Tough day at the office?" she said, holding out a glass of wine to him.

He glanced at the glass in her hand and then up to her face. "What's going on?"

She shrugged. "Just trying to be friendly. The kids are with your mum. I thought we could have a cosy evening together."

A bark of laughter erupted from his mouth. "You're out of your mind." He turned away, heading to the office yet again.

Celeste put the glass of wine on the kitchen bench. "I don't know why you think that. Can't you talk to me? Hug me? Give me one little speck of consideration?"

Mark turned abruptly. "Consideration? You threatened to take the kids away from me."

Celeste blinked. "Did I? When?"

Mark's face changed. His lips curled into a snarl and his cheeks flushed. She saw his hands curl into fists and gaped. "You bloody well know when."

"The kids think you're a robot replacement. I'm beginning to think they're right. Something is very wrong with you. If you were a robot, you'd be a bad robot!"

"You have a bloody nerve." The blow came out of nowhere. She lifted her arm to block it. "Mark! Stop!"

He wasn't moving. He was looking at her, teeth gritted as if ready to strike again. She stared at him, not really noticing him because there was something strange with her arm. He had broken it. Breaking eye contact with him, she lifted it, examining the damage. Exposed skin revealed filaments of nerves, crackling and twitching. She looked closer and those nerves were not what she had thought. There were tiny lights in the break in the flesh and a glint of metal. Before she could digest what she had seen, a hand closed over her throat. "I'm going to strangle the life out of you." The hand tightened. Instinct closed in. Celeste reached out and placed her hands around his throat and squeezed. The hand around her throat dropped away. She lifted him up so his feet couldn't touch the ground. He made choking sounds and the skin of his face above her hand had turned purple.

The door opened. "Hold. Command Celeste One." It was a familiar voice. Her focus was on her attacker, but it was a voice she knew.

Mark struggled against the hold.

"Lower him down, Celeste." Celeste lowered him down. "Thank you," the woman said.

The woman spoke into her phone. "The act of violence is on record. You may come to take him away."

Frozen in place, Celeste listened while the woman organised for Mark to be secured. In a few minutes, he had been sedated, and within half an hour, he had been taken away.

The woman calling the shots stepped into view. She had long blonde hair that fell past her shoulders. Her eyes were pale blue, and her skin was sun blushed to an almost olive. The lips were pink and her teeth perfectly straight and white. She looked just like Celeste. "I'm sorry you had to endure that. I needed to prove that my husband was violent and a threat to me. I had to do it in a way that I would not get killed or injured and I needed to make sure my children were safe."

Celeste listened and calculated all of her recent experience. She was a robot, a tool, and wasn't Celeste, a wife and mother, as she had thought. It was a strange feeling to understand that. Relief and a disconnected sense of disappointment flushed through her system.

"What happens to me now?" she asked.

"Ah," the real Celeste said, nodding slightly. "You're very expensive to keep and the children will be confused if there are two of us. I'm sorry to say that you will be decommissioned and your parts recycled."

"I see." A strange sense of resignation overcame her. *I had been real. I had had a life.* Before she could argue, the real Celeste spoke. "Command Celeste Two."

Celeste grew tired as her energy drained away. Her limbs became heavy, her eyes began to close. Images flashed in her mind, with sounds of laughter and chaos. She would not see the children again. She would not cut lunches or clean the bath. She would not do school drop-offs or the grocery shopping or...

The world went dark and quiet.

* * *

"Dad!" Grace squealed as she ran to the door. "Come and see what I did."

Mark smiled and picked her up, swinging her around. "Sure! I will race you." Grace turned and squealed as she headed back to the lounge room.

Celeste turned and smiled. "Hello, honey! How was your day?"

"Great. And yours?" He leaned over to kiss her on the cheek.

"Great, thanks."

Celeste sipped her wine as she watched her family.

"Now show me what you did. Hey, Jasper." He leaned over and checked the screen on the game his son was playing. "That's a great score. Well done. I'll play you later."

"Sure, Dad."

Celeste dished out the dinner, poured herself another wine and smiled. Mark's robot replacement was all she could've hoped for— a good breadwinner, an excellent father, a great companion, marvellous in bed, and more attentive and considerate than she could have imagined.

No more discontented wife.

AFTERWORD

This has been a fun exercise and a celebration for me. Finally, I'm back at my computer, writing and loving every minute of it. I thought that thrill, that zen zone of creating stories was gone for good. PhD burn out maybe. I'm not sure. I set a goal and I'm meeting my goal so that's also a bit of a buzz. Robot Hearts is here.

This collection came about because I had a couple of older stories sitting in my hard drive gathering eldritch dust and I'd written some new ones last year. I tried to market the new ones to SF magazines and anthologies but no luck and you know that takes a lot of time (months and years) and energy, not including the cut of rejection. I figured if I wrote a few more stories, I'd have a collection so I did. *Happy dance!*

One thing I noted coming through some of these stories is a feminist sentiment. Others are just about how robots serve us, care for us and how we project ourselves onto them.

Thank you to my partner, Matthew Farrer, for reading some of these stories and giving me first reader feedback.

We both write and it's been a pleasure to share this reinvigoration of our writing enthusiasm and zeal.

Thank you to Ian McHugh, my PhD buddy, long-term writer friend and awesome person for editing the collection. Thanks to Jason Nahrung for proofreading the stories and getting all my commas, paragraphs and tenses correct.

Thanks to Angie Rega for always, always being positive and supportive, food preparer and hug giver. Love you. I have a great set of writing buddies Nicole Murphy, Cat Sparks, Kylie Seluka, Leife Shallcross, Kimberley Gaal, Kaaron Warren, Russell Kirkpatrick, Rob Porteous, Chris Andrews and Glenda Larke. There are really too many to name and apologies if I left you out.

Special thanks to Keri Arthur from both Matthew and me for the pep talk that really got us going. That 1000 words a day is a mantra around here. And grateful thanks to Dan Annett and Nik Vincent for the time you took so spend with us, for the mentoring and collegiate creative infusions in Kent.

The Canberra Speculative Fiction Guild (CSFG) continues to mentor and support writers, and I am grateful to them for all the avenues I have to engage in writing and critique. Romance Writers of Australia also provides so much support and professional development and particular thanks goes to Helen Katsinis and the other Paraloopies for support, advice and promotion.

I've hoped you have enjoyed the stories. If so, let me know by sending me a message on my website http://donna mareehanson.com or leave a review or ranking.

Writers need a pat on the head now and then because writing is a solitary job. Alone in our heads, we need a touch of reality and encouragement to keep going.

Importantly, thank you to the readers. You are what a

writer wants and needs. Someone who likes what we do, appreciates our efforts and enjoys our work.

Virtual hugs from me.

Donna Maree Hanson

September 2024

ABOUT THE AUTHOR

Donna Maree Hanson is a traditionally and independently published author of fantasy, science fiction and horror. She also writes paranormal romance under the pseudonym of Dani Kristoff. In April 2015, she was awarded the A. Bertram Chandler Award for 'Outstanding Achievement in Australian Science Fiction' for her work in running science fiction conventions, publishing and broader SF community contribution. Donna writes dark fantasy (the Dragon Wine series), epic fantasy (the Silverlands series), steampunk (the Cry Havoc series) and young adult science fiction (Space Pirate Adventures) as well as short stories across the speculative fiction genre. Her short story collection, Beneath the Floating City was shortlisted for an Aurealis Award in 2017. Her most recent novel, Awakening (2022), is science fiction with romance and the first in a proposed series.

In 2022, Donna completed her PhD candidature, researching Feminism in Popular Romance at the University of Canberra, Her degree was awarded on 30 March 2023. Donna lives in Canberra with her partner and fellow writer Matthew Farrer.

Also by
Donna Maree Hanson

Cry Havoc Series (steampunk fantasy)

Ruby Heart, Cry Havoc Book One

Emerald Fire, Cry Havoc Book Two

Amber Rose, Cry Havoc Book Three (upcoming)

Silverlands Series (Epic Fantasy)

Argenterra: Silversands Book One

Oathbound:Silverlands Book Two

Ungiven Land: Silverlands Book Three

Dragon Wine Series (Dark Fantasy)

Shatterwing: Dragon Wine Part One

Skywatcher: Dragon Wine Part Two

Deathwings: Dragon Wine Part Three

Bloodstorm: Dragon Wine Part Four

Skyfire: Dragon Wine Part Five

Moonfall: Dragon Wine Part Six

Love and Space Pirates (Science Fiction Romance-Sweet level)

Rayessa and the Space Pirates

Rae and Essa's Space Adventures

Opi Battles the Space Pirates

Short story collections

Beneath the Floating City: Short science fiction stories

Through These Eyes: Tales of Magic Realism and Fantasy

Colony Five Series (Science Fiction Romance-Sweet level)

Awakening